# A SEAL FOR CANDACE (SPECIAL FORCES: OPERATION ALPHA)

FIGHTING FOR HOME BOOK 1

JULIA BRIGHT

This book is a work of fiction. Names, characters, places, and incidents are products of the author's imagination or used fictitiously. Any resemblance to actual events or locales or persons living or dead is entirely coincidental.

Dear Readers,

*Welcome to the Special Forces: Operation Alpha Fan-Fiction world!*

If you are new to this amazing world, in a nutshell the author wrote a story using one or more of my characters in it. Sometimes that character has a major role in the story, and other times they are only mentioned briefly. This is perfectly legal and allowable because they are going through Aces Press to publish the story.

This book is entirely the work of the author who wrote it. While I might have assisted with brainstorming and other ideas about which of my characters to use, I didn't have any part in the process or writing or editing the story.

I'm proud and excited that so many authors loved my characters enough that they wanted to write them into their own story. Thank you for supporting them, and me!

READ ON!

Xoxo

Susan Stoker

# CHAPTER 1

Adam "Archer" Culver crossed his arms over his chest as his lip curved up on one side. "I'm sitting over here so I can protect your skinny ass."

Killian "Slayer" Walsh's eyes narrowed, but his expression stayed flat. It took a lot to get Slayer to laugh or frown or do almost anything other than display his resting bitch face. The man was solid on the team, and his lack of expression didn't mean one thing about the depth of his ability to care for teammates.

Dion "Sugar" Washington patted Slayer on the back as he took his seat. Sugar scared people. He had this one look that made you think he was about three seconds from snapping. But when kids were involved, the man was a teddy bear. Every time kids popped up in the group they rescued, Sugar would make sure they were protected and somehow make them laugh. Luckily Sugar knew four languages, which helped keep the kids calm. His parents had sent him to the best of the best schools, hoping he would be a lawyer or doctor, but Sugar had gone into the military and become a SEAL, which was exactly what he told his parents he would do when he graduated high school, much to their chagrin. Sugar spoke to his parents now, but it had taken four years for the truce to come about. By then, Sugar was a SEAL team member.

Archer took a sip of his beer while keeping an eye on the room. He, Sugar, and Slayer were in Georgia for an educational opportunity. They weren't taking classes, instead, they'd spent two days training Homeland Security and FBI agents at the Federal Law Enforcement Training Center in Brunswick. It was a special gig designed to prepare federal agents for the next wave of terrorists. The SEALs had been used to bring weight to the discussion since they were on the front lines, dealing with terrorists overseas.

This was his first time at FLETC, and Archer felt he'd done okay at the training thing, but he was more comfortable in the field running an operation.

The training wasn't something they'd sought out. Instead, it had come down as a command from somewhere up high, and no amount of alternative suggestions they offered got his team out of the training.

Taking a day after to relax was totally Archer's idea. They'd chartered a boat on St. Simons Island and spent the day fishing off the coast while shooting the shit and blowing off steam. The hotel he'd booked was on the island and the bar only two blocks away. The place wasn't too loud, but it was filled with men who had obviously spent the day playing golf and getting way too much sun.

Archer's muscles tightened when some guy stumbled over, slopping beer over his hand and onto the floor as he walked. He looked like he spent more time at a desk than in a gym, and he'd forgotten to apply sunscreen.

"My buddies and I think you're military. I said you were Special Forces, but he believes you're Marines. Now then, if you could settle a bet for us. Which are you? Rangers or Marines?"

"We're not military," Archer said, hoping the guy would walk away. Earlier today had been perfect on the water. They'd planned to fly under the radar and go unnoticed here on St. Simons. Obviously they'd underestimated how drunk and uninhibited these golfers would be after playing a round in the sun.

In San Diego, they weren't bothered by anyone other than girls and a few guys wanting to suck dick or take part in some other naked arrangement. Archer appreciated a good dick sucking, but this guy wouldn't drop to his knees. Besides, Archer didn't swing that way. He didn't mind when guys hit on him. Instead, he took it as a compliment. Women were his thing, and he liked all types, but he didn't want to indulge here where their actions would be remembered for years to come.

"No, no," the guy slurred. "You have to be. I need this win." The man leaned over, and his beer tilted, spilling a bit on Slayer's leg.

Time stilled as Slayer's eyes narrowed and his lips turned down in a frown. Obviously, the man spilling his beer didn't realize Slayer was two hundred and thirty-eight pounds of pure muscle ready to dismantle everything the drunk guy was in ten seconds or less.

Archer wished the drunk away. Thankfully, even Slayer knew they had to stay calm. Being a SEAL meant they had to live to a higher standard, even if some fuckwit in a bar was bothering them.

"Come on, help a guy out. You're military, I know

you are. You must be one of those super-secret teams. What is it? Ranger, Beta, Alpha, or are you a S—"

Slayer's chair screeched as he stood, steam rising as he towered over the drunk idiot. Slayer didn't lay a hand on the man, but he didn't have to. Intimidation was his first language, and he spoke it fluently.

"Turn around, march over to your table, and sit down. Never speak of us again." Slayer's words weren't yelled or said through clenched teeth, but the message was clear.

The drunk man's eyes went wide, then he ducked his head and slunk over to his table. Slayer sat and used a napkin to dab at the beer on his jeans. When he looked up at Archer and Sugar, a full smile spread across his face. Shock filled Archer. Today was the first time he'd ever seen Slayer smile so big.

"Now that was epic." Sugar lifted his beer and clinked it with Archer's. "Never thought I'd see the day you actually gave a full-on teeth-filled grin like some little girl winning a pony. Being here, putting up with the bullshit training we had to do, walking them through scenarios like they were too stupid to figure it out on their own, it was all worth it to see you smile." Sugar took a long swig of his beer, his eyes twinkling with merriment.

Slayer seemed to chuckle before his expression went blank. "How's the baby?"

Sugar beamed. "Momma and baby are doing fine. We're set for delivery in six weeks. I gotta tell ya, I didn't want to be a father at first. Scared the shit out of me. But I'm getting into it now. I'm ready to meet the little bug and see what she's like."

"You're the first of our team," Slayer said between sips of his beer.

"Youngest, too," Archer added. He kept the jealousy from his voice. Archer had been married for about ten minutes—really two years—back in his twenties. They were on the same page, or he thought they were. It turned out she'd lost her sanity while he'd been overseas. He was over it now, but a small part of him wondered how many kids he would have had if she'd stuck around.

"We're happy," Sugar said. "Actually, we're more than just happy, I'm head over heels in love right now."

"Jesus," Slayer said as he took a swig of his beer, the flat expression sticking with a vengeance.

"Can't help it if I've found my one."

Archer chuckled before taking another swig. A few of the other SEALs had been with Molly. When Sugar had come to him a few months ago, worried about being a father, Archer had almost suggested a paternity test. But they were fairly sure Molly hadn't slept around after hooking up with Sugar. She wouldn't downgrade from a SEAL—her words—and all the guys swore they hadn't touched her in months.

Would Archer ever find his one? No other guy on his team had found their one. The six of them were all hard workers, none of them ever balked at their missions, they all took their jobs seriously and went above and beyond what was expected. He never questioned if any of them deserved to be on the team. They'd all passed BUD/s, which meant they earned the team and much more. But finding a partner who would put up with their crazy lives was hard.

His buddy, Matthew Steel, had found gold when he'd met his one. It seemed like almost everyone on Steel's team had gotten lucky in the love department. Most SEALs didn't make out so easily. Divorce rates were eighty to ninety percent in the ranks. It was rough going all around. SEALs expected too much from their partners. The disparities between expectation and deliverables were daunting when every single day you lived giving your one hundred percent. Archer knew it was unfair to put those demands on civilians, but the reality of his life was he had to stay on task every minute of every day or forfeit his life. Civilians didn't understand the intensity burning in his veins, and it was unfair to expect the same from them.

They finished their beers without anyone else talking to them and then headed back to the hotel. Their flight was early, so partying was out. Not that they would party on this sleepy little island. It wasn't Berlin or LA. This town was small, and any activity outside of normal family-friendly behavior would be shunned or remembered.

Like every other night of his life, he went through the list of people he was thankful for, which included his dad, who had put a cigarette out on Archer's back when he was nine, telling him it would make him stronger. It had, and now his dad was dust in the wind since Archer had refused to pay for a burial. The bastard got what he deserved, dying alone in a shack where hookers wouldn't even go.

The next morning he and the guys were at the airport, ready to board their plane home when he got the call. Some bozo had ambushed a group of soldiers in Iraq and taken them over the border into Iran. Diplomatic channels were being exercised, but his team was being deployed to fix the situation if some politician couldn't talk the Iranian government into giving up their people.

Archer hated this kind of shit. He just wanted people to get along but was wise enough to know it wouldn't happen in his lifetime. Archer didn't have faith in others to get life right, so he'd become a SEAL to help them when they went astray. Usually that help came in the form of a bullet to their brain, but he trusted himself to make those tough decisions.

His ethics and morals were straight in his mind. That he had to kill people to get the job done didn't faze him. What did bother him was lowlifes taking advantage of weaker individuals. This mission might end with a few Iranians dead, but it was a price they would pay for taking what wasn't theirs.

# CHAPTER 2

Candace Cunningham fumed as she waited for one of the men she was with to grow some balls. They'd been taken twenty-four hours ago, and not one of the guys had tried to come up with a plan. The three of them had shot her down as soon as she'd opened her mouth to lay out an escape plan.

"Mike, your ass isn't the one getting raped once these knuckle draggers get bored," she whispered, her words harsh.

Mike scoffed. "I'm not risking my life for you."

Anger filled her. She'd risked her life for them time and time again. This time, they'd been joking around, playing with a snake amongst the rocks when she'd told them they needed to leave. Fourteen of them had gone out, five had played with the stupid snake, and only four of them were left.

Mike had been playing around, and now they were stuck here in some falling down house, being held prisoner by lunatics.

"Shut up, Candy," Greg said.

He was just as bad as Mike. How she'd gotten paired with this group, she didn't know. It had to have been bad luck, possibly some Karma for some slight she'd tossed out in high school. Or perhaps this was punishment for the guys she'd broken up with because they didn't live up to her standards. She'd been an insufferable prick before she joined the military. Mike and Greg probably thought she was still insufferable, but she'd just wanted them to live.

The door opened and she shrank against the wall, praying they ignored her. Usually, she would kick ass without even thinking of taking names, but she had no weapons and no way to defend herself.

They were speaking Farsi, which she didn't understand. Had they been speaking Arabic, Kurdish, French, German, or English, she would have known what they wanted, but she didn't understand enough Farsi to catch what they had planned.

The jerks grabbed her, and not one of the guys with her did anything or said anything.

"Stop!" Candace yelled.

Someone's hand flew and smacked her across the face. She tried to pull away but was kicked from behind. Her legs went out from under her as the enemy dragged her from the room. She screamed and fought, scratching and clawing until they knocked her out.

Sometime later she came to, alone in a room on a cot. She wouldn't shed any tears right now. Pain slid up her spine when she moved, but she could move. They may have tried to break her, but it would take more than what they gave to get her to fold. Later, once she was rescued, she would cry about her situation. For now, she would kick ass, or try to. The jerks would have to kill her to get her to stop fighting. She found her clothes and pulled them on, hands shaking as pain almost pulled her under.

Once dressed, she found her way to the hall. No one was there guarding the room. She shouldn't go looking for trouble, but she was sick of being taken advantage of by assholes who had no discipline and no morals.

Voices floated down the hall. She rushed to a door, finding it unlocked. Her heart raced as she stepped in. The room was pitch black. Fear wrapped around her throat, choking her. Her respiration rate increased, and she had to force herself to calm down.

The voices in the hall grew louder then quieted as they passed. She slid down the flat surface of the door and wrapped her arms around her knees. No escape and no help. Crying sucked, but everything came together, swamping her. One tear slid down her cheek and she swiped it away, but more came, running down her cheeks in little streams. Fuck them and fuck their country. Bitterness filled her. She wanted to go home.

She must have drifted off at some point and woke to the sound of people running in the hall. Time had little meaning since they'd been taken. The voices grew louder. Her throat squeezed as fear filled her. She jumped up but had nowhere to go. If she stayed in this room, she would end up being found, but if she left the room, the risks were wide open.

The decision was taken from her when the door burst open. Two of the guys who had raped her grabbed her arms and pulled her out into the hall. They shouted as they dragged her, not allowing her to get her feet underneath her so she could walk. She pulled at their hold, fighting as she vowed to never give in.

They shoved her into a chair and held her down while one guy grabbed her hand. She screamed, fighting to get free. Punches to the side of her head made her stop screaming for a moment, but she wouldn't stop fighting. They would get no satisfaction from her giving in to their demands. They would have to take her by force if they wanted her.

One of the punches took her breath away. She blinked, then squinted as the guy holding her hand strapped it down and forced one finger out. He lifted his hand and swung it down on hers.

For a second, she didn't register what had happened. Then pain so sharp she almost peed her pants raced from her hand, up her arm, catching her on fire. The wailing started, and in some part of her brain, she knew it was her doing the screaming.

He hit her again.

It was a hammer.

*Oh God, so much pain!*

The crunch of bone was almost deafening as the hammer slammed against her hand again and then again. The asshole kept at it, beating her hand until pain enveloped her. She almost passed out, or she did, she wasn't sure.

Relief came when they stopped hitting her. Then they came at her with a white-hot poker. The guy shoved it at the end of one of her fingers. She opened her mouth and screamed so loud her eardrums ached.

Candace wanted the black of oblivion to take over. The pain fried her nerves. Her mind fogged, but she stayed with them. They were yelling at her, waving the hammer at her, screaming and hollering. She had no idea what they were saying. Would they kill her now? At least then, her pain would be less.

# CHAPTER 3

Archer checked his watch. He had two hours until their plane landed. He hated the distances they needed to travel just to do this rescue. The other SEAL team in the area was on a mission deep in Pakistan and couldn't be called out. There were other Special Forces teams, but with the issues in Asia, the war raging in Africa, a group needed in South America, and he didn't even want to get into the mess in Syria, there were few options. It just sucked how it took so long to fly halfway around the world.

If life grew more complicated, another SEAL team would be forced to deploy, thus having two teams in a war zone instead of one. It might increase the number of SEALs and thus increase the teams. It wasn't just the six guys who deployed when they were assigned to be somewhere like Afghanistan or Iraq for six months. Hundreds of people traveled with them from commanders to support staff. The United States hedged their bets, counting on the plan two operations wouldn't have to be run at the same time. It was a risky maneuver, leaving them open for attacks like the one they were on a mission to rectify today.

Liam "Flip" McClanahan stepped close and took the seat next to Archer. "You get any more intel on this op?"

"They are in a house on the edge of town. It's a hovel, more than a house. They do have two big guns we have to take out." Archer had little doubt Flip had a plan going in his mind.

"I'll check for satellite views," Flip said. "I'd like to take Mist on the field trip with me."

Zachary "Mist" Fennel could shoot the eraser off a pencil. He knew Mist would keep Flip safe as he went in to destroy their big guns.

"Sure. Take Mist and Sugar. We need to move fast. The sun will be down in two hours once we land on the carrier."

Once on the ground, they would take a helicopter to an aircraft carrier and then transport from the carrier to a Combat Rubber Raiding Craft. The CRRC would take them into Iran, which was a violation of some accord and would get them in deep shit if Iran found out. But Iran had their people, and enough time had passed without giving them up that the military decided the diplomatic solutions wouldn't work.

"Did you sleep?" Flip asked.

"A bit," he shrugged. "I'm good to go."

"Cool. I'll have a plan ready before we land."

He nodded as Flip stepped away. The team was waking up, looking at their email, preparing for the operation. Mist sat up suddenly as the plane bounced. His blue eyes were wide, his lips thinned. When he realized nothing had happened other than a little turbulence, he rested against the seat and closed his eyes.

Archer knew how Mist felt. They were trained to wake up, ready to do whatever needed to be done. A few of the guys had some PTSD. They knew they needed to take care of mental health, but it was a tricky line to walk. If you said you wanted to talk to a psychologist above and beyond what was considered regulation, you might be benched. To go out on operations, you had to be okay. But it didn't mean you didn't need more time to talk through things with a professional. Sometimes talking wasn't enough to get over the things they'd seen.

The plane landed, and Cole "Black" Kennedy was the first off. Cole had everything under control. No doubt, the young lieutenant would get his own team soon. Archer would hate not to have Cole on his team, but the man was freaking amazing and deserved to lead.

"You ready to party?" Mist asked as he passed by Archer.

Mist had just come back from one week off for a funeral. The man hadn't said anything when he got back, but Archer noticed the changes. Archer knew from his personnel file Mist had changed his name from Zachariah to Zachary when he turned eighteen. Archer also knew Mist had grown up in a cult but escaped. He'd fought to get his life on a path he chose, and the man had won. When he'd first expressed interest in becoming a SEAL, many tried to tell him he wouldn't make it, but Mist pressed on, graduating at the top of this class. Archer expected great things from him.

They hopped onto a helicopter and flew out to the carrier. After a quick briefing, the team loaded into the CRRC. The sun had set, and clouds blocked the moon. It would take them four hours to get to the house where the American soldiers were being held. He prayed they were still alive when they got there.

Time passed quickly on the water and then as they made their way into town. They had positioned themselves two blocks away from the house where the US soldiers were being held. Flip, Mist, and Sugar had moved ahead to plant explosive devices on the two artillery guns set up beside the house. Everyone on the team was ready to move in one minute. The explosive devices would be used once they were all clear. They didn't have to blow up the guns, but he didn't want this group to have any big weapons left after they vacated the area.

It would draw attention, but if Mist and Flip set the charges correctly, which he knew they would, the explosions would point to the group in the house screwing up, not a SEAL team demolition.

"Bravo two to Bravo one," Flip said over the communication devices. "We're ready to go."

"Bravo One, we're moving in." Archer's heart picked up speed for a short moment, then he forced himself to calm as he stepped closer to the door to the house where the Marines were being held.

Slayer set up to breach the door. Every member

had a task, and without hesitation, Archer trusted them to do the job they'd been assigned.

Archer flashed his hand, showing three fingers. He folded one in, then the next. When he folded in his last finger, Slayer moved, crashing open the door. Mist tossed in a flashbang seconds before they filed in, each of them taking a side of the room, scanning, searching for enemies. One unlucky soul ran toward them. Sugar took him out.

There was yelling, someone screamed, and chaos seemed to rule the house, but Archer's team moved like a well-oiled machine. They took out four combatants before they found the room where the Marines were being held. There were only three of them. Disappointment wove through Archer. He'd been led to believe there were more. The two women in the group must have died.

"Bravo Six to Bravo One, I'm clearing the back of the house," Mist said.

"Bravo Four to Bravo One," Slayer voiced. "The front of the house is clear."

"Sounds like—"

"Oh shit."

Archer waited for a second to determine who had spoken. He recognized their voices, but random conversation during the middle of an operation didn't usually happen.

"Bravo One to whoever said that, what is going on?"

"Sorry. Bravo Five to Bravo One, I've found one of ours, I think," Sugar said. "She's in a bad way, but the tattoo on her back means she isn't one of theirs."

"Shit," someone whispered.

"Bravo Five, I'm headed your way." Archer moved through the house, trusting Flip to secure the Marines and get them moving.

Down the hall and in the last room, he found Sugar bent over a naked woman. She had blood on her back. Her pale flesh was flayed like she'd been whipped. Her tattered tattoo of the American flag showed plain as day. She wasn't one of the terrorists' women. Instead, she was one of the women from the Marines.

"Bravo One to Bravo six, you're needed back here."

Flaming hot anger twisted in his guts as he stared at the shredded tattoo. No mistaking it was the Stars and Stripes, but the wielder of the whip had used enough force to tear it up. If any of the men in the house were still alive, he would kill them, but they were already put down like the dogs they were.

Because they were in Iran, they had no over-watch. Going in without support was risky, but they had few options.

They had the four surviving members of the Marine unit, but now they had to get out without attracting attention. Having an injured person in the mix sucked.

"Can she be moved," Archer asked Mist the second he showed up.

Mist took about thirty seconds, then nodded.

"Good. Get some clothes on her," Archer growled.

"Yes, sir." Mist moved fast, finding a shirt and pants for the woman before he scooped her up.

Mist was built like a brick and had endurance out the wazoo. He would handle carrying this woman without asking for help, but Archer would make sure they switched people at some point in the click they had to traverse to the shore where their CRRC was stowed. It wouldn't take them long. Hopefully, they would get out of Iran without drawing any attention to themselves.

"Bravo Two to Bravo One," Flip said. "I'm setting the charges to go off in five minutes."

"That gives us plenty of time. We should be far

enough away, and no one will look for us." Archer felt good about this mission. "Let's move out."

His good feelings turned sour when the Marines they'd come to rescue moved so slowly he wasn't sure they'd be away from the town when the explosive devices went off.

"Move it," Archer barked. The guys grumbled, but Archer wasn't having any of it. "Get your ass in gear."

They were halfway to the beach when the buildings exploded. The woman slung over Mist's shoulder moaned. Archer ached for her. She had a load of recovery just from the physical stuff, who knows what mental torture she'd have to face once home.

He asked Mist if he needed relief, but he declined, saying they were moving so slow that carrying this woman was like a walk in the park. Once in the CRRC, he turned to Mist. "Tell me how she's doing."

Mist stared down at her. "She won't die right now, but she's hurting. Look at this." Mist held up her hand, showing the broken mess and the stump of one of her fingers. The hand looked infected.

"Shit," Archer said.

"Yeah, shit."

They were approaching the carrier when the woman started to wake. The first thing she did was let out a scream. Archer moved fast, covering her mouth. She struggled against him until his words broke through.

"You're safe. I'm US military," he repeated for the fifth time.

He'd bent close enough to see her wide eyes and pinched brow. She had to be in pain. The mental war going on inside her brain showed in the distrust shining in her eyes and the way her gaze shifted to the other men in the CRRC.

"About time you rescue me," she said loud enough the rest of the guys chuckled.

"You're safe now," Archer said.

"How many did you rescue?" she asked.

"There are four of you."

They hit a bigger wave as they approached the stern dock of the aircraft carrier. "Fuck," She said as a cough racked her body.

"You can talk later. Rest now." Archer placed his hand on her shoulder, trying not to apply pressure and hurt her. She cringed, but he didn't let go. She reached for his hand and squeezed his fingers, gasping in pain as they hit another wave.

Archer met her gaze and held it. She needed to

feel grounded, even if it was on this tiny boat with strangers. The pain she'd experienced was exposed in her gaze, and his heart squeezed. He wanted to help her more, but they delivered her safe to this ship, and it was someone else's job to care for her. Maybe she had family back home, perhaps even a husband. She would get the help she needed.

They tied off at the stern dock of the carrier, and the men they rescued were ushered up. A stretcher was lowered for the woman, and the medics from the ship took over. Archer wanted to ask for more information about her, but she wasn't his concern any longer.

He and the rest of the SEALs were led into a briefing room and given food, something to drink, and told where to change and freshen up.

Thirty minutes later, after he'd showered and changed clothes, he stepped out of the briefing room and ran into a Lieutenant Commander. Archer saluted, and the man waved him off.

"Good job out there, Master Chief Culver. I'm impressed with your team. Actually, even our Rear Admiral is impressed, and he never tells any of us we've done a great job.

"Thank you, sir." Archer glanced at his name. It was Walbusen. "It's my pleasure to serve."

"I'm sure it is. You SEAL boys take great pleasure in wreaking havoc."

"The woman we rescued. Will she be okay?"

Walbusen shrugged. "Who knows? Physically her body will heal, but she went through hell. She is a fighter. I just came from the medic bay. She has defensive wounds on her arms and legs. She took hell, but she gave it back, too."

Archer's shoulders tightened as he thought of her fighting for her life. He prayed she took the fight home with her. She would need it to recover from the hell they'd put her through.

After doing a quick briefing with Washington, they boarded a helicopter and started their trek back to the United States. They slept on the plane, then when he was bored with sleep, he caught up on email, answering questions and pressing send though he knew the email wouldn't send until they were stateside.

His mind drifted to the woman with the shredded Stars and Stripes tattoo. She had a lot of healing ahead of her, and she may never fully recover. He just hoped she'd dished out enough pain before his team killed those men.

# CHAPTER 4

The plane landed in San Diego. She was here to meet with a hand specialist and to talk to a post-traumatic expert. Candace clenched, then opened her good hand, still lacking the ability to squeeze her injured hand or use her fingers. The mess of the bones and ligaments looked frightening, and the space where her finger was gone bugged the heck out of her. She hadn't only lost a finger; she'd lost so much more when they'd captured and beat her.

Two months had passed since her rescue. The Marines had offered her a medical discharge because when she'd tried to go back to work, the damage both physically and mentally was too much. She didn't want to stop being a Marine, but staying in wasn't an option.

She grabbed her bag, wincing as the strap scraped over the scars on her back. The fuckers had whipped her without mercy, ripping the skin off as they'd beat her for some made-up infraction.

Hard tears had fallen when she'd gotten a good look at her tattoo. The piece had meant the world to her. Her best buddy, Axel, had designed the tattoo for her. Two months after she'd received the ink, he'd died in Afghanistan. Anger had mixed with the pain, twisting everything in her mind. She wanted to get over it all, but she wasn't sure she ever would.

Candace caught a Lyft to her hotel and checked in, wishing she felt brave enough to go out and sightsee. Her confidence was shot, and she wasn't sure she would ever get it back. The one bright point of the whole trip was the SEAL team who had rescued her had agreed to meet with her. The missing time needed to be accounted for, and maybe the SEALs could help. When she'd woken up in the Zodiac, she'd been disoriented as hell. All she knew was some big bear of a guy had been in her face, telling her she would live.

The first morning in San Diego, she headed to the hospital to start in on the appointments. First, her blood was drawn, then she headed over to the cafeteria for coffee and food. After she'd replenished herself, she went to the doctor's office and sat for almost an hour. Since returning to the States, she'd spent too many hours in hospitals and doctor's offices, waiting for someone to call her back to a tiny room where she could wait more. She'd tried reading, knitting was out of the question. She'd played games on her phone, and she'd even tried writing about her experience, but nothing calmed her mind enough to keep her from freaking out. The best thing was to sit and stare straight ahead and force herself not to have a panic attack.

"Cunningham, Brock, and Edwards, come on back," a woman called out.

Candace stood and moved to the doorway where the nurse waited. The two other people stepped over, and they were led into separate rooms. Candace figured she would have to wait an hour or so before the doctor came in, but it was only a few minutes before the door opened, and a young man stepped in followed by a nurse.

"Hello, I'm Doctor McKinzy. I've been doing hands for a while. I understand you have an issue. Tell me what happened."

She hesitated, trying to stay in the right frame of mind as she spoke of her torture. "Um, I was captured by the enemy, and they hammered off my finger then sealed the wound with a hot iron. They also broke some bones."

The doctor moved closer and rolled a metal table in front of him. "Could you place your hand on the table?"

"Sure." She lifted her hand, her mind spinning over what she'd told the doctor. Would he treat her differently because she'd been captured? Did he know she'd been raped repeatedly by those men?

Shame shifted through her as the doctor stared at her hand. She was about to hop up and leave when he met her gaze.

"From the looks of it, they tried to destroy you. I'm glad you're strong enough to have survived. This had to have hurt like hell. There are a couple of things I'd like to do. First, I want to open you up and do some surgery to fix the bones. I looked at the X-rays from the other hospital, and I can do better, which is why they sent you out here. Second, I'd like to do a skin graft from somewhere else onto the end of your finger. It would hurt, but the skin would look nicer, and it wouldn't be the burned skin we have here. It would extend your recovery time by about six weeks, but in a year, the skin would feel and look better."

His words almost physically hurt. Maybe it

wasn't his words, but the memory they invoked. She'd almost wanted them to chop off her hand when she'd come home. It was a painful reminder of what they had done. If this doctor did a graft, would it look normal or closer to normal? He lifted his eyebrows like he was encouraging her. She blew out a breath.

"I don't know what to say."

"I specialize in hands, but I've been here for a few years. Though I look young, I'm almost forty. I've seen a lot. There are a lot of men and women who come home missing parts of their bodies. It's normal to have fears. I've done a few hundred skin grafts, not like yours, but close. It takes time to heal the graft and the rest of the work I will do. I'm not going to lie, the skin graft will be painful, but in a year or two, it will look more normal. It's up to you, but you need to have the bone cleaned up, and you need to have some other work done to fix your hand, or at least make it more usable."

She nodded as she stared at her hand. The nurse hadn't said anything yet. It was hard to know what to say. She'd endured hell, and now she had to live through the aftereffects. No civilian would understand what she'd been through. Maybe someone who'd been a victim of a horrible crime over here would get it, but most of those people died. Heck, she probably should have died, but she'd been found, and perhaps her life wasn't worth the price they'd paid to find her, but she was forever grateful.

"Okay, let's do it."

"Awesome. We'll get you scheduled. It'll probably be a week or two out. Where are you staying while you're out here?"

"I was in a hotel by the airport last night. Tonight I move to a hotel that is for veterans. I have a room there for a few weeks and can extend it up to a few months depending on treatments here."

"Good. I hope you have time to enjoy the city and the beaches before surgery. Once we operate, you'll have to rest for a while because of the skin graft."

She nodded, unsure about the graft. "Sounds good to me."

"Okay," the nurse said. "Let's get you set up for surgery."

It took another forty minutes to get everything set up. Then came her therapy session with the psychologist. It wasn't as bad as she'd assumed it would be. The woman, Cynthia Baker, didn't push her too hard. They would start doing Eye Movement Desensitization and Reprocessing therapy soon. She was nervous about the EMDR therapy but needed to do something to move on and have healing because living with the hell in her head was driving her crazy.

After she arrived at the new location where she was staying, she received an email from the person coordinating her meeting with the SEALs. They would meet her on Saturday at noon. She had an address, and all she needed to do was go. Her heart sped up and sweat popped out on her brow. Would talking to the SEALs be too much? She slid down the wall and watched the shadows move across the room as the sun sank lower. Paralyzing fear took over, and she didn't even go out to eat. She wanted to get better, but she had a long road ahead. Maybe once she knew how the SEALs had found her, everything would calm down.

# CHAPTER 5

Candace had surgery scheduled in eight days and would be in the hospital for two nights. The hospital stay didn't bug her as much as the sessions with the psychologist. Working through her issues was akin to pulling out her fingernails with pliers.

The hole in her memory for those hours when the SEALs found her bugged the heck out of her. She wanted to remember everything so she would never be haunted by the fear of what happened again. The scars across her back gave a clue, but what else had happened when she'd been unconscious? Maybe how the SEALs found her would help to fill in the missing time.

Her alarm rang on Saturday morning sometime around nine. She rolled from the bed, surprised she'd slept so late. Since leaving the military, she'd wanted to stop waking at the crack of dawn but hadn't been able to sleep late at home. She was happy she'd been able to stay in bed until well after the sun was up. It had to be the intense sessions she'd had with the therapist and the start of the EMDR therapy that allowed her to sleep.

After her run, which was more like a jog, she showered then dressed. Twice she thought of canceling. This had the potential to heal a hole in her mind, or it would rip her to shreds. She wanted peace, but what she wanted more was to never have gone through any of the torture in the first place.

Her hired driver arrived, and for a moment she considered giving him a five and telling him to leave her, but she got into the car, buckled herself in, and sat with her good hand clenched in her lap.

At the first light, the driver turned and looked at her. "You fight in the military?"

The words shocked her. She sucked in a breath as memories hit hard. "I…uh."

The light turned green, and he took off. Saved by the light. Candace blew out a breath, hoping she could face these men. She wanted a blow by blow account of everything. From the moment they showed up until she was on the ship, she needed to know what had happened.

The car stopped. She wasn't ready, but staying in this car, answering questions by this guy she didn't know, was impossible.

"Thank you." She shoved a five-dollar bill into his hand and jumped out, slamming the door before she moved closer to the bar. Aces was the name, but she was too nervous to wonder what the history of the place was.

Her throat dried as she stepped in. The place was mostly empty since it was early in the day. The bartender was a man, about fifty years old, who reminded her of her dad. Tears burned her eyes as he waved. It wasn't her father. She wouldn't ever see the man who raised her again. Her heart ached for all they'd had. If he'd still been living, maybe what had happened wouldn't be so bad.

"Candace." The word rumbled over her, causing her knees to turn to jelly. She spun and gawked at the guy.

He was huge, like a beast. His brown facial hair was trimmed neatly with a hard line under his cheekbones. His dark hair was wavy and longer than the guys in the Marines. But no doubt, he was military based on how he stood, totally aware of everything and ready to attack at any moment. His lips were full and wide, and she bet if he laughed it would be loud. She wanted to see him smile. Why had that thought popped into her mind?

"I'm Adam Culver, the lead for the team who rescued you. We're all in here if you'd like to come in."

"Th-thank you." Her feet were heavy, almost like she had on concrete shoes as she stepped closer to him.

"Would you like something to drink?" Adam's voice was low. His dark eyes stayed on her, but she had the feeling that if someone burst through the front door, this man would know who it was and have them assessed in less than two seconds.

"Just water?"

"Are you sure? Jim, the bartender, makes a great tea."

She looked over her shoulder then back to Adam. "I haven't had any alcohol since I've been home. I'm a little afraid of being impaired."

"It's okay. How about I get you some water and tea? It's peach blackberry today." Adam walked over to the bar and spoke with the man. Jim was what Adam had called him.

She stood in the middle of the room, awkwardness seeping through. Another man stepped into view and flashed her a smile. He seemed monstrous, too. Fear wove through her. This had been a bad idea.

"I'm Black, well, Cole is my name, but everyone calls me Black. You can come on back. We ordered some appetizers because we're always hungry, and we weren't sure if you would want to eat or not."

She glanced at Adam then nodded. "Okay."

Her body shook as she stepped deeper into the restaurant. The four still sitting looked imposing. One of the guys hit her with an icy stare, and she may have flinched. The guy stood and flashed her a grin, making him look a little less threatening.

"That's Slayer," Cole said. "He's really nice, but he looks like he's ready to kill. Comes in handy in our line of work."

"You all are being good, right?" Archer asked as he stepped into the room. He set the water and tea down and motioned for her to sit. He hadn't remembered her being so small, but it had been two months ago. She looked wary, like she wanted to bolt. Adam hoped the guys wouldn't scare her. Images of her from the night they'd found her filled his mind. He had to force them away. She probably had a horror show of shit flowing through her mind every night and didn't need more reminders.

"Eat up," Black said as he grabbed a few nachos from the plate in the center and took a bite.

Archer wanted to tell Cole to be more polite, but they were all hungry. They'd gone for a run then played volleyball until an hour before they had to be here. None of them had time to grab food, which meant they wanted to eat. The rest of the guys started grabbing nachos, and Slayer got up.

"Where are you going?" Black asked.

"Get more food," Slayer called over his shoulder.

"I don't eat much," Candace said. "You don't need to get more."

"We eat a lot." Archer studied her, taking in her soft brown eyes and her thin lips. Worry lines criss-crossed her forehead. He wanted to reach up and smooth them down, but he didn't dare touch her. Just sitting beside her was enough to get him warm. He needed to stop. She didn't want some horny guy hitting on her. That wasn't why she was here.

Candace's tongue was too huge to talk as she stared around the table. Overwhelmed wasn't how she wanted to be, but something was keeping her from opening up. She guessed it was fear. She wanted information but a part of her feared knowing. What would be worse? Did she really want to know the nitty-gritty?

"How is your visit out here going?" Cole asked after he swallowed the overflowing nacho he'd bitten into.

Her stomach rumbled. She was a little hungry, but her nerves would keep her from enjoying the food. "Um, I've been at the doctor's office for most of it." She glanced down at her hand, hating the sight of the missing finger and the melted skin and all the other issues making her hand look terrible. She'd already had one surgery when she'd first flew home, but she needed so much more to fix the wreck. This new surgery couldn't come soon enough. She had hidden her hand from strangers, not wanting questions. At a grocery store, before she'd come out here, some kid had seen her hand. He'd been frightened. She didn't blame him. What had happened to her was awful.

"How is that going?" Adam asked.

She shrugged. "Okay, I guess. I have surgery in eight days. Right now, I'm going through EMDR." Her therapist was good. She liked her, and the therapy seemed to be helping, but she had a lot to go through.

"It's good therapy," Cole said between bites. "I know a few guys who have had great success."

"I hope it helps. Right now, it's tough just to live. I have a hole in my memories of what happened. That's why I'm here. I want to know what happened. Where was I when you all found me?"

Silence fell around the table as the guys stared at their drinks. Her head ached and her stomach churned. When she'd woken up in the military hospital, the doctor had told her she'd been raped. The confirmation had almost been too much. Thank goodness she'd gotten on a long-term solution for birth control before traveling overseas.

For a part of the rapes, she'd been unconscious, but a whisper of a memory taunted her when she closed her eyes. A shiver snaked through her, and though she tried to suppress it, she wasn't successful.

Candace's face scrunched up and Archer could tell her distress rose. What they'd seen had haunted him for weeks. The memory was one he hoped would go away forever. He'd talked about it with the psychologist he went to after the mission, but the image had stuck around. He understood Candace's desire to know everything. If he found himself unable to remember chunks of time, he'd want a blow by blow account of every minute he'd been out.

Candace seemed skittish. It was good she'd found a therapist doing EMDR. Loads of military men and women were finding help with the therapy. He just hoped Candace received relief.

A large part of him wanted to pull her into his arms and hold her, but she wasn't his. Did she have someone to hold her on long nights when the fear became too much? He imagined some guy trying to comfort her, and the sizzle of jealousy burned in his belly. Why did he care if she had someone at home? The woman wasn't his and he didn't know her. But he wanted to know her, which had him questioning his sanity.

The heat of Adam's stare settled on Candace. She glanced his way and noticed warmth flashing in his eyes. What was that about? There wasn't any way this hot SEAL was interested in her. She was just some pathetic person they'd rescued and not dating material. She had to focus on recovery, not finding someone to lean on. Standing on her own two feet and taking care of herself was important. She figured part of taking care of herself was figuring out what had happened in the lost hours in her mind. A few had warned her against knowing, but that chunk of missing time haunted her.

"I found you," the guy across the table from her stated.

She met his gaze and held it. His dark eyes drooped a little as sadness took over his expression. A sliver of fear twisted through her. They didn't want to talk about finding her. It was evident by the way they had dodged the question and avoided her gaze.

The man who'd found her was big with a serious look on his face. His hair was black and short, though it was longer than the black guys in the Marines wore theirs, he still looked clean cut with no facial hair compared to the other SEALs.

"I'm Dion Washington. I was the one who found you."

She swallowed over the rising fear. What terrible things had they seen when they'd rescued her? None of them were volunteering information, so she would have to pry it out of them. "What happened to me?"

"Ma'am, I don't know what happened," Dion said.

Of course, they didn't know what had happened. They weren't psychic, but she'd hoped they would have some insight. She was grasping at straws. The need to know everything wove through her. But what if knowing made things worse?

Candace swallowed over the fear and leaned forward, praying this man had a clue what had happened before she'd been rescued.

"Anything you know, I just need something." She sounded desperate to her own ears.

Dion swallowed then nodded slowly. "It's graphic."

"I need to know," she begged.

"Okay. When I found you, you weren't wearing any clothes, and you'd been whipped. You were face down on the ground, bleeding from multiple wounds."

Her vision narrowed in on Dion. Everything else faded away. She'd heard his words but was having trouble digesting them. How many times had those men raped her? She craved the details, thinking they would help her close off that part of her mind and stop worrying about it.

"Were they raping me when you came in?" The question flew from her mouth. This was difficult, but she needed to know. It was like some desperate driving force was pushing her.

Archer shifted uncomfortably in his seat. Candace shot her gaze his way. Pain fired in her eyes. Was that guilt he saw? She didn't feel guilty, did she? Anger for her flashed through him.

The freedom to have a say had been taken from her. His guys didn't want to speak about how they'd found her. They'd unpacked the scene enough times for him to know it bugged them all. Seeing Candace on the ground, blood oozing from her wounds had disturbed them.

"We had killed them all by the time we found you." Archer's words sounded stiff. Had one of the terrorists been in the room with Candace, he probably would have ripped them to shreds. "None of the men escaped, and none of them were taken into custody. They all died.

Candace blinked at him, seeming almost like she didn't see him. She shook her head and breathed out a sigh of relief. "Oh."

The urge to pull her into his arms struck Archer again. The rest of the guys were here, but that wasn't the only reason he stopped. She didn't need some jerk mooning over her. Candace deserved to have some peace in her life. He hoped the therapy helped.

Pain flared at Adam's words. Candace stared at her glass of tea, wishing she had asked for something stronger. Suddenly she wanted to get drunk and say to hell with everything.

"We found clothes and dressed you before we

took you out to the ship," Adam said. "The other Marines we rescued weren't in the room with you."

At least those assholes hadn't seen her naked. She didn't hate the guys she'd served with, but she wasn't friends with them. If they'd been there when she'd been raped, she wasn't sure they would have stood up for her. She moved to get up, but Adam put his hand on her arm.

"Don't go yet. We'd like to spend some time with you."

Her lips thinned as worry spread. What did these men think of her? She'd been used by those monsters, and though she was trying to get past it, she hadn't overcome the worst of the abuse she'd suffered.

"You need to eat," Adam said.

Right then, a plate of potato skins with bacon on top was delivered to the table. It smelled so good that her mouth watered. She'd planned on heading back to the room where she was staying and hiding, but they got her with the bacon. It would be rude to leave with bacon on a plate in front of her.

"Here, have some," Cole said as he placed two potato skins and some nachos on her plate.

Hunger won out. She took the first bite, moaning at the taste. She hadn't been eating enough food. Her clothes were loose and her energy low. Maybe with the therapy, she would start eating again. The food tasted great, but still, worry consumed her.

The guys started talking about baseball and how they wanted to play on a softball team this year if they got the chance. Adam kept glancing at her. Warmth spread over her face and down her neck when their gazes caught.

Adam leaned in and asked, "You doing okay?"

She nodded then shook her head. "I don't know."

"We've all seen some scary shit," Cole said.

"I was taken hostage for a week. I'm Liam. It was before I became a SEAL. I wasn't tortured like you were, but it scared the shit out of me. I thought I might die. I had to work to get over it. When I was in BUD/s, the training to become a SEAL, I almost dropped because they were trying to get into my head."

Candace stared at Liam for a solid thirty seconds. He seemed so strong. She prayed for strength. "How did you get the voices out of your head?"

"It took therapy and time. Also activity," Liam said.

She ducked her head, sadness filling in all the empty spots. "When I was at the hotel, it was too much. I didn't even eat dinner because I was too afraid to leave the room."

"I'm sorry," Liam said. "It's tough. The mental stuff is more difficult than physical injuries."

She nodded, sadness flowing. "I feel like the mental stuff will take forever."

"How long are you in town?" Dion asked.

"For a while." Her words sounded hollow.

"You don't seem thrilled," Adam said.

Candace shrugged. "I don't know how to deal with it."

"What do you mean?" Adam asked.

She'd said too much. These guys didn't want to know how she'd lost weight after leaving the Marines because of fear. She feared going out, feared having to deal with other people, feared what people would say or do. If she kept at it, her life would be fear and nothing more.

# CHAPTER 6

Archer's heart went out to Candace. The hurt in her eyes tugged at him. They had almost destroyed her when they'd captured her. She hadn't answered his question, but he didn't want to keep pushing. He wanted another chance to talk with her. Maybe he was making too much of the connection, but the idea of getting to know her intrigued him.

The guys kept talking, most of them sharing funny stories, trying to lighten the mood. By the end of the hour, Candace was calling them all by name and seemed happier. Archer liked seeing her smile. It made his day.

Sugar received a text and had to go. Then Flip and Slayer took off. Mist left after those two, which only left Black at the table with the two of them.

"I should go," Candace said.

"How about you call if you're afraid to go get food. I could talk you through it." A thread of panic wove through Archer. Suggesting she contact him again was out of character. It was rare they met with the people they rescued. They'd only met with her because her rescue had affected their team. They'd freed captured Marines, Army, Air Force, and Navy guys as well as civilians, but for some reason, Candace had struck a chord with them. She drew out something inside. Perhaps it was her tattered tattoo, or the few words she'd said before the medics on the carrier had taken her away.

Her brows bunched, and she shook her head. "No, that's asking too much of you."

"No, it's not. I'd like to help." Adam watched her face, hoping she would give in.

"Seriously. You need a good support network," Black said. "I know I can call on my guys. What about you? Who are the people you can call on?"

A shiver snaked through her and Archer wanted to reach out and pull her into his arms. She looked so sad.

The truth sucked. It was something she'd been avoiding, but she wouldn't lie to these guys. "Everyone close is dead."

"What do you mean? What about those guys who we rescued you with?" Black asked.

Pain flashed, and she rolled her eyes. "Those guys were jerks. They—" She stopped talking, worried what they would think.

Adam took her good hand and rubbed his thumb over her palm. "Tell us."

She closed her eyes, trying to block out the pain. It didn't help. "They were fucking around, which is why we got caught. Then while we were in the house, they didn't even try to get free or anything. I mean, I know we have to take care of ourselves, but those three didn't seem to care I was being tortured."

"That sucks. I know my guys will die for me," Black said. "Of course, I'd die for them. Not everyone is cut out for military life."

"What about your buddies? Surely there's someone for you from your Marine unit?" Adam asked.

The truth of the matter sucked worse than anything she'd ever known. "No, actually, there isn't. A few months before I was captured, Axel, my best friend in the Marines, was killed. Actually, all of my friends were killed. Fifty of them all at once. It was terrible."

"Oh shit, I remember that," Archer said. "It was in Afghanistan, right?"

"Yeah. I'd stayed on base that morning to take care of a special assignment for the colonel. I was devastated."

Archer's stomach twisted in knots. He'd lost a few friends, but not everyone. The Marines had taken a hit recently with helicopter crashes and ambushes. He wouldn't be able to make it if his guys all died.

"Why were you still deployed after such a tragedy?" Black asked.

Archer wanted the question answered, too. Why had they allowed her to stay on deployment? She should have been sent home. Losing a unit was difficult for those who survived. If they'd been thinking, they would have given her a few months to recover. Candace seemed stronger than most, which made sense with everything he knew about her, but still, so much loss took its toll.

"I was moved to another unit that was deploying. They didn't think it through or they didn't care. I had a hard time adjusting to my new group. The guys I was with didn't care for me, and I wasn't a fan of theirs."

She'd had more than just a hard time adjusting. It

had been hell getting used to the new unit. Maybe she'd taken things too seriously with the deaths of her friends, but they hadn't taken the war zone seriously enough."

"That settles it," Adam said.

"What?" Candace was curious. These men were good people. She hadn't really known them, but they were acting like she fit in. It felt good and made her sad at the same time. She'd fit in with her unit that had been killed, but not so much since then. She wanted to belong but wasn't open enough to find a new group of friends on her own.

Adam's smile spread wide. "We'll be there for you."

She shook her head, and Adam held up his hand. Black reached over from where he was sitting and took her hand.

"We're here to help."

She stared from Black to Adam, worried she would rely on them too much, and they'd want her gone. They needed to be warned how screwed up she was, but Adam gave her a silencing glance.

"Please trust us."

She gave a slow nod, worried they would dump her once they realized what a colossal dork she was. "Okay, if you're up for it."

"We are," Archer said.

Their concern gave her a boost. Perhaps there was hope she would make it. Therapy was hard, and she wasn't looking forward to another surgery, but she needed to recover and this was part of it.

"Now then," Archer said. "Let me have your phone. I'll enter my number."

She pulled her phone from her pocket and opened it before handing it to him. She looked nervous, like she wouldn't call him, but he planned on checking in with her. After he entered his phone number, he dialed his own phone. Now he had her number, too. Black took the phone next and entered his number. Though Archer wanted her to call him if she was having issues, he wouldn't complain if she called Black. Or he wouldn't complain to her. He wanted her to have someone to reach out to. The idea of her being out there, too upset to go get food because fear overrode her good senses, made his worry increase.

"Thank you," she said as she tucked her phone into her pocket.

"We're here for you," Black said as he stood. "I have to get back to the house but thank you for meeting with us."

Candace pushed her chair out and rose. Archer

stood and held out his hand. When their palms touched a spark slid through him. “Thank you.” He tried to keep his voice even, but he sounded like a teenager trying to impress some hot girl in his class.

Candace seemed too small to be a Marine, too small to be out there taking risks he knew she had to have taken. She’d made it through basic and had survived being captured. Many badass guys he knew wouldn’t survive what she’d been through. Her size wasn’t indicative of ability. Some SEALs were smaller but were strong as hell. Candace had to be strong. Maybe she’d lost weight after being abducted.

Black strolled out, waving at Jim as he went. Candace glanced up at him then looked away quickly. She crossed her arms over her chest and wrapped her good hand around her upper arm. Her fingers dug into the muscles of her arms, making her knuckles white. The last thing he wanted was for her to feel threatened in his presence. He took a step away and smiled at her, hoping she didn’t see him as a threat.

She glanced around, worrying her lower lip with her teeth. “I guess I should head back.”

“Would you like a ride?” he offered, praying she said yes.

"No, I can take a cab or a Lyft."

Her riding with a stranger set him off. He followed her out to the street, both of them blinking and shielding their eyes from the harsh sun after being inside the dark bar.

She had her phone out, the application for a ride pulled up. Her hand shook as she entered the address. The desire to pull her into his arms and take care of her struck so hard he had to clench his fists. She glanced up as he grunted. He softened his expression and tried for a smile. Her lips twitched up, and her brown eyes warmed for just a second before she glanced away.

"If you need someone to talk to, call me," Archer said. "I'm serious about being there when you need it."

She nodded, but he worried she didn't believe him. Her gaze went back to her phone as she finished entering the information. The words "Promise to call me," died in his mouth. She wasn't his.

He'd dated around since his fiasco of a relationship in his early twenties, never again settling down. If a woman got too serious, he would step away because the last thing he wanted was to be tied down again. Back before he'd become a SEAL, he'd been cocky, but his interest in Candace wasn't because of some cocky ego he had going, he wanted to have a relationship with her. She was his, she just didn't know it. Which meant she wasn't his, and if he wanted more with her, he'd have to work damn hard. Did he have time for a real relationship?

Candace wanted to take Adam up on his offer to drive her home, but she didn't want to be a pain in his ass. Already, she'd taken up most of his day. When she looked at him, he was staring openly at her. Heat rose up her chest and neck, filling her face.

There was no way he was interested in someone like her. Not beautiful or smart, she was average at best. The idiots overseas had damaged her. She had too much wrong with her life for anyone as amazing as Adam to give a second glance.

"The car will be here in a few minutes. I'm okay." She hoped she sounded confident. Before everything had happened, she'd been different, better or at least more confident. Hesitating on little things made her worry she would hesitate on big things. Ultimately it was why she'd left the Marines. Her judgment and her reactions were off. She hesitated on everything.

"I'm not leaving until I know you're in a safe car, and I can trust you'll get back to the location where you're staying."

Adam's words warmed her. She knew he was a good guy but having him care about her enough to stay for a few minutes made her tingly inside. Her cheeks turned pink based on how hot they were. Tears gathered in her eyes before she ducked her chin. He placed his fingers under her chin, and she lifted her head to meet his gaze.

"Hey, what's up?" Archer asked.

His concern was almost too much. Candace had been running on empty, and now she had this good looking, kind man concerned about her. Why had he even given her a second thought? Worry hit hard, and she bit her lower lip.

Archer didn't like this. Candace needed to find happiness. He wasn't sure he was the man to give it to her, so he didn't lean in and kiss her though he wanted to. He also didn't back away, obeying the warning in his brain.

Candace was a keeper, not someone to toy with and walk away from. If he decided to go after her, this would be for keeps.

She shook her head and then sucked in a ragged breath. "Nothing is up. It's stupid."

He touched her shoulder, realizing he needed more touches from her. "I bet it's not."

Again she wrapped her arms over her stomach,

holding herself tight. "Axel, my best friend, he would say stuff like that to me."

"Is he one of the ones gone?"

"Yeah. He's the one who designed my tattoo." A sob escaped her lips. She closed her eyes, and her face crumpled in a mask of pain.

Archer wrapped his arms around her shoulder and pulled her to him. He didn't know how else to soothe her or even if it was possible. She'd lost so much, and the cracks hadn't healed at all.

A car pulled up beside them. He let go and stepped away. It was the hardest thing he'd done in ages. It took a force of will to not haul her into his arms and take her with him. She needed so much, and it hurt to let her walk away.

She met his gaze, her lips trembling. "Thank you."

"You're welcome. And call me later."

She nodded, but he feared she wouldn't call. He memorized the license plate and made a note of it before she got too far. The urge to hop into his truck and follow her hit but trailing her would be too stalkerish.

All the way home, he wanted to call her. The desire stayed with him as he did yard work and cleaned his house. Archer had stayed in base housing longer than he'd been required. Now he lived in his own home, which he'd paid a considerable chunk down, making the payments low. His pay in the military wasn't huge, but he'd invested wisely and received enough hazard pay to live comfortably even in California.

After he finished cleaning inside, he dropped to his favorite patio chair, beer in hand, as he stared at his phone, willing it to ring. Should he call? Usually, he was sure of himself, but he hadn't challenged himself in the dating department in a long time. It was easy for him to find babes who wanted some SEAL action. He hadn't had to work for anything with a woman in years. But Candace was different. If he developed anything past friendship with her, he would want it to last. And that scared the crap out of him because lasting relationships for Special Forces guys were rarer than four-star generals and full bar admirals who didn't have their heads up their asses.

# CHAPTER 7

Candace shook as the shouting continued. She'd been woken up when the screaming had started, and no one was doing anything to stop it. Someone slammed a door, and more screaming ensued. She dropped to the floor and slid over to the corner. Her arms were wrapped tight around her legs as she rocked and hummed, trying to drown out the sounds.

The awful house, the yelling, the men touching her all came back. Tears filled her eyes as her mind spun. She fought the demons, trying to gain a grip, but she was close to spiraling out of control.

Candace grabbed her phone and opened it to call the cops and let them deal with this. The last person she should call was Adam. His name swam before her eyes. Somehow she made it to the screen to share her location. Talking would be too hard. Even typing a message explaining her desperation was too difficult.

Three seconds passed, then her phone rang. The people outside her room ramped it up as she answered.

"Hello—what is that noise?"

"Adam?" Her voice shook as she spoke.

"Shit. I'll be there in a moment. Let me…the map says it will take me fifteen minutes. Don't hang up."

Something squeaked like a bed on the other end of the line, then water ran. It was comforting listening to Adam move around his house. A door opened then a vehicle engine roared to life. The shouting continued, and Candace curled into a tighter ball.

"You still there?"

"Y-yes." She slammed her eyes closed, fighting to concentrate on his voice.

"I'm going to sing while I drive."

Music started, and she turned up the volume. Adam's deep voice resonated through her. He wasn't perfect, and he wouldn't ever be on stage, but he was the best singer she'd ever heard. He kept her from losing her mind as the people yelled at each other.

"I'm here, Candace. Go to your door and open it."

Unwrapping her arms from around her knees was difficult. She stood on shaky legs, flinching when the person yelled for the millionth time.

"I'm right here, just keep moving," Adam encouraged.

She took another step, then another. Finally, she was at the door. She spun the lock and pulled the door, falling into Adam's arms.

He picked her up and carried her inside. The screaming continued. Adam grunted then moved to the bed, setting her down.

Archer couldn't believe the people outside. They were having a full-blown fight in the middle of the night. Why hadn't anyone called the cops? Anger filled him, and he had the urge to open the window and tell them to shut up, but this wasn't his fight to deal with. He and Candace weren't sticking around. Instead, they were headed to his place where she would sleep in his spare bedroom.

The idea of Candace at his house made him happy. He wanted her with him, but this wasn't exactly how he'd planned on getting her close. He hated the panicked look on her face and how she kept eyeing the wall where the screaming was coming from.

Adam got her attention and lifted his brow. Her features relaxed a bit. He wanted to celebrate, but he still needed to get her to safety.

"Your things. What do you need?"

The screaming started again, and a pained look crossed her face. Panic shone in her eyes. He moved fast and had her rucksack out, taking her clothes and folding them into the main compartment. He moved to the bathroom and grabbed her bag there, making sure everything was packed inside before he zipped it closed. With her bathroom cleared out, he checked the plugs for cords. They were good to go.

"Did I miss anything?"

The look on her face made his heart squeeze. Going back to before she'd been taken captive was impossible, but he would protect her from more horror.

Candace glanced around, her mind still a little fuzzy as she searched the room. "I don't know."

"The place looks clean. I don't see anything else you left out. You didn't stuff anything into a weird place, did you?"

Candace shook her head, grateful Adam would help her. "No."

He picked up her bag and then her before he carried her out to his truck. Though she could have walked, she didn't complain. Instead, she clung to him, holding on until he placed her in the truck. He strapped her in and she didn't even flinch when the door shut beside her.

They were four stoplights away from the place where she'd been staying before it really sunk in they were gone. A bubble of hope filled her. Was this really happening? So much had happened in the last few months. It only took an argument from strangers to wipe out the progress she'd made and send her back into a tailspin. If Adam hadn't been here for her, she would have lost hope. She would have gone on to self-harm or something else destructive if he'd not come to rescue her.

Candace turned to look at Adam. He appeared serious, maybe even angry. Was he pissed she'd called? She could find another hotel but staying in the room she'd been in was out of the question.

"Where are we going?" Candace asked.

"I have a guest room. I have to be at the base at seven tomorrow, but I'll be home by noon. Do you have doctor appointments tomorrow?"

She blinked at him, trying to remember her schedule. "No. It's Sunday."

"True. Don't leave my place. That's not a suggestion, that's an order."

Orders she understood. "Yes, sir."

Adam pulled into the driveway of a small house. The porch light illuminated the front yard, showing off the beautiful flowerbed. The house was painted blue with white trim and had a small porch out front. The one tree in the front yard looked nicely trimmed. Did this lot have a back yard and would it be nice?

It was late, and the traffic had almost been nonexistent. She should have paid more attention to where they'd driven, but she was happy just to hold herself together and not freak out.

She opened the door of the truck and slid out, landing on the small strip of pavement below. The sound of the freeway wasn't too bad, and the neighborhood was quiet, unlike the place where she'd been staying.

Adam came around and took her hand, leading her into his house. He shut the door, and the noise from outside died down. The lights flipped on, revealing a clean den with a couch and a recliner across from a TV on the wall with speakers flanking it. The kitchen was small, but he'd utilized all the space and had stored his pans over the sink on a chrome ring.

"I don't have any pets. During the day, it's safe to

sit outside. Nighttime is okay as far as safety goes, but it is a big city. The back yard is more comfortable than the front. I leave the windows open if the weather is nice and I'm here. Otherwise, I lock it up tight. The guest room is through here. I have a meeting first thing in the morning, but I should be done before lunch. There is an alarm for when I travel, but I rarely set it when I'm here."

She glanced around, taking in the place. Adam didn't have a lot of extra stuff, but there were a few books on a shelf and some intriguing paintings. Her gaze fell on him, eliciting a smile.

"You're too nice. You didn't need to do this."

He gave his head a short shake. "Bullshit. All the yelling, how were you supposed to get any sleep?"

Guilt started working on her. "I'll search for another place to stay."

Adam stepped close. He bent his knees, trying to get his face to her level. He looked ridiculous, so she tilted her head up to look at him.

"I'm happy to help you. This place is quiet all the time. My neighbors are good people. The area is safe, well as safe as a huge city can be. You can hang out on the back porch. It gets sun in the morning and is in the shade during the afternoon when it's hot. It seriously is one of my favorite places to be. You can rest and heal."

She bit her lower lip. His offer was too good to be true. "I'll have surgery and won't be able to do much."

Archer usually didn't have anyone stay with him, certainly not a woman. He had the guest room set up for when his buddies flew into town. Otherwise, the room was empty. He didn't want a roommate, but with Candace, he wanted her to stay for a long while.

"If you're not capable after surgery, then I can wait on you while I'm home. I may have another mission I have to go on, I'm not sure. I'll do what I can, though."

Her gaze slid away from his. He wanted to reach out and make her look at him but touching her would be rude. She finally glanced back at him and gave him a half-smile.

"Are you sure? Won't me being here be a lot?"

"I'm positive I want you here." Adam hoped he hadn't revealed too much with his statement. He should have said it another way. "And you'll have me close by. If something happens, I'll be right in my room or outside. I have to be at the base most days at seven or so, and I finish around three unless we have something go down."

"Like having to rescue someone like me," Candace quipped.

Candace didn't need someone drooling over her. The woman needed time to heal, and him being a jerk wouldn't help her. He hadn't had someone live with him for years. Even when he was on base, he had a private room. A couple of his friends would come and stay one night, maybe two, but those visits were few and far between. They weren't regulars who stayed weeks. From what Candace said, it looked like it would be weeks or a month.

Could he take someone in his space for a month? He would find out soon enough. He adapted well in most situations he had to. This would be another adaptation he'd have to make.

He cupped her cheek and smoothed his thumb over her skin. "Trust me, no one is like you."

Her heart kicked up a notch, and for a second she believed he would kiss her, but he stepped away and moved to a short hall. He was too nice. She risked falling for him if he didn't stop it.

"The bedrooms are back here." Adam pointed down a long hall. "There is one full bath. Trust me, I don't take long in the shower unless it's after a mission, then I take a bath and have a beer while I relax."

She grabbed her bag and followed him to the back of the house where he opened a door and led her into a small bedroom. The bed looked comfortable, and the place was decorated nicely.

"This is the guest room. I don't get too many guests, so the room is yours. Oh, and there is a half bath behind the kitchen on the way out. Sometimes I forget to stock it with toilet paper. You need to check in there."

"Thank you. You're too nice. I may be in San Diego for a few months."

His lips turned up in a smile. "I'm good with you staying here. I enjoy having someone to talk to at times. I mean, I'm fairly quiet, and I don't chat with everyone like Black, but I'm not Slayer."

"Black, that was Cole?"

"Yes."

"Slayer, was?"

"Killian. He's a good guy, just quiet."

"That's right." She placed her bag on the floor and looked up at him, seeing the kindness in his eyes. She wanted to talk more, but he had to be at base by seven, and it was almost midnight. "Thank you. Sleeping here will be better. I really appreciate it."

"Sure, and any food you want, take it. I'll be heading to the commissary tomorrow afternoon. We can shop then."

"Thank you."

He pulled her into a quick hug, leaving her wanting more. The room was clean, with no dust on anything. It was exactly what she would expect from a Navy guy. She pulled her clothes from the bag and unpacked. She folded her rucksack and shoved it in the bottom of the closet before she found the bathroom.

Once back in the guest room, she kicked off her shoes and socks then pulled her jeans down before slipping off her shirt. She grabbed a loose shirt to sleep in and settled in the bed. Adam was too nice. Comfortable in this room, she relaxed. It had been so long. The number of good days and good nights were so few she could count them on one hand.

She rolled to her side and clutched the pillow, sighing as the pressure in her head and in her chest eased up. She woke late the next day and pulled on her jeans, not waiting to run into Adam unless she was dressed. Based on how quiet the place was, she figured he'd already left for base.

After taking a quick shower, she checked outside. His truck was gone. She grabbed an apple from the refrigerator and headed to the back yard with a cup of coffee. The morning sun warmed her skin.

Once she finished her apple and coffee, she stretched out in the chaise lounge and must have fallen asleep. She woke to find Adam staring at her.

"Hey," she said as she sat up.

"How are you feeling?"

"Good. Thank you. I don't know what I would have done if I had stayed there."

"Thank goodness you didn't have to. The guys are planning on playing volleyball on the beach. Want to join us?"

She appreciated how he didn't feel the need to stay with her all day. She was having surgery and would have to keep her hand dry and clean for a few weeks until the skin graft healed. Maybe a trip to the beach was what she needed. Fresh air would do her some good.

"Um, sure. I won't play, but some sun would be nice."

"Awesome. Let me change. Do you have a suit you want to wear?"

She shook her head. "No." The scars were too much to show. She may never want to go without a shirt covering her top again. The messed-up tattoo bugged the heck out of her. It would be a year or more before the scars would settle enough for a tattoo repair. She didn't want to destroy it or cover it up, she just wanted it to look nice again.

"Okay. I'll be ready in five minutes."

She nodded and headed to her room to grab a pair of sandals and a bottle of sunscreen. She pulled on some shorts and a different shirt. Before leaving the bedroom, she grabbed a book she'd bought at the airport on the way out here. She hadn't gotten into the book, but it was by an author she used to read before she joined the Marines. So much had changed since joining up. She was proud to have served, but the cost she'd paid was too much. She doubted she'd ever be the same person again, if she even wanted to be that person. Being abducted had changed so much. She'd been upset by losing her friends, and then she'd been taken captive and abused. Being held, not knowing if anyone would rescue her had been nightmarish. When Adam and his group had taken her from the hell overseas, she'd been surprised someone had come to help. Maybe she was worth saving.

She stepped into the main room and noticed Adam had grabbed a few bottles of water, some chips, stuff for sandwiches, and fruit. The drive to the beach only took fifteen minutes. When they parked, she hadn't worked up the courage to talk about anything.

The beach wasn't too crowded. Adam had brought a chair for her, and she watched for a while, read a little of her book, and then closed her eyes and relaxed.

Everyone from Adam's SEAL team was there except Dion. The guys played hard for almost an hour before taking a break. Then Dion showed up with his pregnant wife.

"Hi, I'm Molly. Dion's wife," the woman said as she stepped close. Her wide smile was welcoming and made Candace feel a little better.

"Hello. I'm Candace."

"It's nice to meet you," Molly glanced around before pointing to the water. "Would you like to walk out to the water's edge? I want to get my toes wet. Actually, I need to ice my ankles. I keep getting swollen feet, and I'm tired of soaking them at home. The cold water will feel perfect."

Candace glanced at Adam, who waved and gave her a slight chin lift. The move made her insides tighten, and her face heated. "Sure." She turned to follow Molly. They ambled toward the water, Molly stopping every few feet to take a breath before she started walking again.

"When are you due?" Candace contemplated what it would be like to have a kid. Stress was the only thing she could come up with. First, her life had to be in order, then perhaps she would consider it.

"Five weeks. I'm excited. I can't wait to hold her in my arms."

Children, husbands, even lovers seemed so far off for Candace. They made it to the waterline and then the guys ran over. Dion ran up and kissed his wife while the rest of the guys dove into the water. Her eyes were drawn to Adam. The man was fine with his chiseled muscles and wide jaw, but he was too good for her. There was no way she would ever find a man like him. If she was lucky, she would find someone who was nice.

Dion ran up to Molly and picked her up. She squealed and slapped at his shoulders as he spun them around. Candace chuckled then turned as a weird feeling twisted through her. She walked about ten feet, maybe twenty, down the beach, unsure about everything. The fight to keep her mind from turning to the trauma she'd suffered was ongoing. She had to keep pushing away the anger. She wanted the pain to be over, but it kept coming back to haunt her.

Archer watched Candace wander down the

beach. The area was safe with the Navy base so close, but he kept his eyes on her. She wasn't cloying like some women he'd dated. She didn't seem to mind getting sandy or being out in the sun. He'd been with women who demanded all his time and didn't want him having fun with the guys. Candace wasn't like that. His curiosity about her grew. What had her past been like and what did she want from life?

Was he getting in too deep? No question, he wanted her. He wanted to find out what foods she liked, her favorite color, what type of flowers she liked, and how she slept. When he walked out onto his patio and found her sleeping in his lounger, he'd had to stop himself from reaching out and touching her. She'd looked so beautiful, peaceful, and perfect.

There was something about her drawing him in. Usually, he didn't care much beyond sex. He was kind when he dated, but beyond the date, he didn't really think about women. He'd never cared enough to ask a woman what type of flower she liked or what her favorite food was. With Candace, he planned on knowing every little thing about her.

Archer patted Flip on the back and ran after Candace. Her body was beautiful, but it was more than just lust pumping through his veins. If she were any other woman, he wouldn't put in the effort, but with Candace, it was worth the time to get to know her.

"Hey, why the long face?" Archer asked as he came up beside her.

Candace bit her lower lip and then sighed. "It's nothing."

The heaviness of her sigh had him worried. "Doesn't look like nothing."

She tried to smile but failed miserably. "I'm dealing with it."

His heart squeezed, and he reached for her hand. "You don't have to deal alone."

Candace wanted to believe him, but she had a hard time believing anyone else cared enough to listen to her fears. Plus, what would they do if they knew how she felt? It wasn't like anyone could take away the pain inside. Then there was the fact she didn't know how to start. And worse, she feared if she did start, she wouldn't know how to stop the flow of fears and worries.

Liam raced over and did a cartwheel in the sand before landing with his hands in the air like an Olympic gymnast. "Hey, time to eat. Come on up. I have a huge blanket."

She chuckled as Liam raced off. Adam moved her closer and his hip brushed against her. She glanced up, seeing heat in his dark brown eyes. Fire licked up her spine and twisted around her belly. She almost squirmed. Adam squeezed her hand and lifted his brows as if to ask if holding hands was okay. She answered by squeezing his hand tighter.

The man oozed safety and security. They were two qualities she hadn't needed until after everything had happened. Now she craved them. Her therapist said she would get better, but until she had her life under control, she would need help navigating everyday activities.

Spending time with Adam and his friends made her heart lighter. The day had been good. When she stretched out in bed, she actually felt more like herself than she had in ages. The clawing feeling in her stomach had lessened, and her mind didn't spin on the what-ifs about being attacked.

Adam was up early in the morning for work. She had doctor appointments and otherwise enjoyed spending time in Adam's back yard. They'd stopped by the commissary to pick up food after the beach. It had been a fast shopping trip, with her telling Adam she didn't need much and him buying it anyway.

On Tuesday she decided to cook something for him for dinner. The chicken was almost done, and the small pasta dish she'd made was warming on a burner when he walked in.

"Oh my, the food smells delicious." Adam stepped into the kitchen and moved close to her, but not touching.

Her face heated as shyness took over. "It's just a little something."

"It smells great, and I'm starving. We ran ten miles this afternoon and then did a full workout. This is so much better than the takeout I'd planned on ordering."

His hand smoothed over her shoulder, then he backed away and headed to the bathroom. He returned in the kitchen after a few minutes, his smile wide.

"Your surgery is on Friday, right?" Archer was amazed Candace had cooked for him. He needed to do more to make her feel safe. He had a few ideas, but he needed to run them by her first.

Candace nodded before she answered. "Yes."

Desire filled him, but it was too soon for touching and hugging. They weren't a couple yet, though he wanted to be. "I'll get the day off and take you to the hospital."

She turned to face him, her eyes full of wonder. "You don't have to."

He cupped her cheek and smoothed his thumb over her soft skin. Desire hit hard and he wanted to do more than touch. His dreams had been filled with her as the star, but sex had to wait.

"Trust me, with all the extra days I get, I have enough time. I'd like to be there for you. Then you'll know who is dropping you off and who is picking you up."

A load of emotions flitted over her face. She seemed worried and possibly angry. He understood both emotions. Change was difficult. When trauma happened, it took a lot to recover. He'd seen it time and time again with his friends. The psychologist Candace was seeing might be able to help her get through the issues. At least he hoped she would. It sucked how evil people were to each other. If there were more SEAL teams, maybe there would be less trauma in the world, but even SEALs couldn't stop everyone.

"I have to be at the hospital early."

He reached out and squeezed her shoulder. "I'm happy to get up and get you there."

"Thank you." Relief filled Candace. Adam would get her to the hospital. It was a huge relief.

"You're welcome."

Adam's smile made her warm. He was a good

man. At first, when she'd called him and he'd come over to get her from the hell where she'd been staying, she'd feared he had ulterior motives, now she knew he was just a good person.

"Therapy is helping," Candace said. "I still have a long way to go. This surgery may set me back emotionally, but I'm happy I came out here for this surgeon. He's an expert on hands."

"That's good to hear. I'm glad he's a competent doctor."

Her body heated at what she wanted to say next. "I'm also happy I met you—well, you all."

He lifted his eyebrows, causing her to heat even more. She ducked her head, and then his feet were in her field of view. She looked up and then took a chance, placing her fingers on his chest.

"I'm thrilled I've been able to spend time with you."

Last night she'd woken from an erotic dream about Adam. They hadn't done more than hold hands, and here she was thinking they might have more than just friendship. But worry still held her. Maybe it was the wrong time to get involved.

Adam cupped her cheeks then stepped closer. His hold was gentle, and she could have moved away at any point, but she didn't want to. She stepped even closer and licked her lips, anticipating their kiss.

Her eyes fell closed just before he brushed his lips over hers. It was magic and fairy dust mixed in with a swirl of panic and lust. She gasped, and he let go of her face before wrapping his arms around her, pulling her closer.

"I can stop if you want," Adam whispered.

She stilled as memories wafted over her. "I'm okay with just kissing. I don't—" a sob escaped her lips.

"I won't ever push you past what you want. I can just hold you later while we watch TV. We can take this slow."

She nodded and stepped out of the circle of his arms. Pain flared, and she reached out, grabbing his arm. "Sorry. I don't mean to send mixed messages. I want to touch you for a few more seconds to make sure this is real."

His lips spread into a smile. "It's real, darling."

She closed her eyes and leaned her head against his shoulder. "You're real."

"I am. And I'm here for you."

This man was too good to be true. She wasn't ready for a full relationship with sex and everything, but it was nice to be held. He was too nice to her.

Candace leaned back and stared into Adam's eyes, knowing she would never live up to what he deserved. She wouldn't walk away but when he realized how much of a loser she was, she would run and never look back.

# CHAPTER 8

The pain in Candace's eyes chilled him to the bone. On Thursday, he came home to find her asleep on the recliner. He didn't want to disturb her, so he headed to his room and changed before coming out.

She sat up and wiped her face when he reentered the room. "Oh no. I didn't cook dinner."

"How about we order a pizza? You've been cooking so much for me. You need the rest."

She chuckled and shook her head. "I'll be resting in the hospital for a couple of days."

"True. But being in the hospital can be exhausting. They'll wake you up at odd times and force you to take your temperature and all that other stuff."

Her stomach grumbled and they both chuckled. "Pizza does sound good."

"Awesome." He grew serious as he stared at her. "Now for the tough questions. Do you hate anything on pizza?"

Her lips quirked up. "I'm not a fan of pineapples or anchovies."

He blew out a breath. "That's a relief. Neither am I."

It was good to joke with her. Before she left the room, she stepped close and hugged him. His heart sang at her touch. She was just right in his arms and just right in his life. When he'd first brought her to his place to live, he hadn't thought they would end up together like this. This was a huge bonus he hadn't expected to happen. She was beautiful, and he wanted to spend time with her, but being in a relationship was tricky as a SEAL. He'd have to make sure she understood work meant long times away, and it was dangerous, which she knew, but he and his team were competent. They would have to deploy, but it wasn't just deploying that would take them overseas. They had to go where needed when they were needed. The things they dealt with would destroy others, but they had to compartmentalize while on a mission, then they had to unpack. It was a balance civilians didn't always understand. Maybe

Candace being a Marine meant she would understand.

If they kept working toward a relationship, they would have sex. He wanted Candace, dreamed of being with her and had woken more than once to dreams of making love to her. But she wasn't ready.

Since they hadn't hooked up, he'd hoped his emotions would stay detached, but they hadn't. This was complicated, and he prayed they worked their relationship out. For now, they were developing a good friendship. He wanted their friendship to stick, even if they never did more physically.

He liked sex, and it had its place, but he'd used sex to keep emotionally distant from women in the past. Now it seemed like if he and Candace got together, it would be a swirl of emotions and connections, bringing them closer. The big question was did he want that closeness with anyone?

He placed the order for pizza, then went out to the back yard and checked the bushes and flowers. His yard was a haven with tall trellises with ivy and flowers in pots, some hanging from the trellis. The city was unforgiving, harsh with lots of hard surfaces. His yard was a place he relaxed. It was his decompression spot to unwind after a long day or a hard mission.

The door opened, and he turned to find Candace. Her brown hair was pulled up in a bun, her face clean of makeup. He liked that he could see the slight blush on her cheeks. Her skin looked touchably soft. She wore a pair of mid-thigh-length shorts and a green t-shirt she'd picked up in the Marines. Maybe she hadn't tried to look sexy, but the woman was the picture of hot sex and lazy afternoons. He wanted her in his bed.

"Your back yard is beautiful. I like sitting out here after my sessions and drinking in the atmosphere."

"Thank you. When I bought the house, it was just a dirt lot. I planted grass, the vines, the flowers, all of it. I don't have much space, but I've made it mine."

"It's beautiful. Really, it's like a park. I love it."

Her compliment made his heart sing. His house was his haven, a calm place where he could relax. He never wanted to live like he'd grown up. Throwing dishes, breaking furniture, it was overrated. God forbid he have someone who would toss a chair at him. Some guys liked crazy, but not him. Cool, calm, and collected were his favorite "C" words. Based on how he'd grown up, who would blame him? Living crazy as a child had given him focus in his adult life.

"The pizza should be here soon."

"Good. I'm actually hungry. Though I am nervous about surgery."

"What time do we have to be there?"

"Seven in the morning. I can't have anything to eat or drink after midnight."

He chuckled. "I've never had surgery, but I have to do those blood draws with no food. A few of them have been close to noon. I hate those days. I'll set my alarm later, and I won't brew coffee."

"You don't have to do that."

"I'm not drinking coffee and eating breakfast in front of you. They'll take you back, and then I'll go get breakfast."

Her heart swelled. This man was too good to be true. This last week had been amazing. How had she existed, not knowing Adam? He had changed her outlook on life. He may not even be aware of how much hope he'd given her.

She knew her sessions with the therapist were helping, but this man, with his calm demeanor and sweet personality, had helped her trust again. Sure, Adam was intense, but he didn't fly off the handle, and he didn't yell or scream. He was strong, smart, and kind, and just what she needed.

"I appreciate you taking me to the hospital."

He moved to her and wrapped her in a hug.

Candace didn't balk at his touch. Instead, she leaned in, wanting his caresses and his kisses, but full on sex was still too much. Maybe after the surgery, and after she healed more, she could enjoy sex.

"I'm here for you."

She shivered at his whispered words, and he leaned in, brushing his lips over her cheek just as the chime of the doorbell filtered outside. Hunger clawed at her, but she wished the pizza delivery would have waited a little longer. Another kiss from Adam would have been nice. Later, they would have time to kiss and hold each other.

"Pizza is here." He planted a quick kiss on her head before stepping inside to get the pizza. He'd wanted to pull her into his arms and make love, but she wasn't ready yet. She needed time to heal, and he wanted the time to grow a real relationship.

Living in California had taken some getting used to. In some ways, it reminded him of the tiny house he and his mother had lived in after his father had been arrested the third or fourth time. His mom always returned to his dad, which made his life hell. But she had no money and few job prospects. The first time his dad beat him after Adam had spent the summer learning karate from their new neighbor who had lived in Korea, his father learned a lesson. It had changed the dynamics of their family. His mom had been angry, but Adam had prevented her from getting beaten worse, and he'd turned the tables, getting in good hits on the old man who used to mop the floor with him.

"The pizza smells great," Candace said, interrupting his memories.

"Dig in." Adam pushed away the sadness as he took his first bite. He didn't want to dwell on his past and how terrible his family had been.

He turned on a movie. Candace dropped down a few inches away from him, but by the end of the film, she was up against his side, tucked in close, and he had his arm around her. He enjoyed holding her.

They had only kissed a few times but watching this movie with her was more sensual than some sex sessions he'd had with other women. After the movie ended, he pulled her in for a kiss. She seemed nervous about the surgery, forgetting to draw away after a few of the heavier kisses.

Being with her would take patience. She had been abused, most likely raped by those men, though he hadn't asked her what she knew had happened. Though she would have scars from the experience, he still wanted her.

A part of him wanted to know everything she'd

suffered, but it wouldn't be healthy to obsess over it. She'd been through so much, he needed to help her heal, not relive the experience.

* * *

The drive to the hospital made her stomach ache. Maybe it wasn't just the drive, but the lack of food. She was nervous as heck, and she needed something to calm her stomach, but she couldn't take anything.

Adam was great. He sat with her until she had been given something to make her drowsy. Before he'd left, he'd leaned over her bed and kissed her forehead.

"I'll be around when you wake up. You're safe."

He'd known she needed reassurance. Not that she doubted she was safe on American soil, but even with the knowledge the terrorist couldn't get to her, she had been nervous about going under. The doctor had assured her she would be safe, but having Adam say it meant the world.

After her surgery, he'd been there in recovery, but she'd passed out soon after and stayed under. He went home to sleep since he needed to be at the base in the morning. Not having her at his place was weird. He did his work at the base and had a long workout session with his team, but he still missed Candace. When he picked her up on Sunday afternoon, she was still high from painkillers.

He helped her get settled in the recliner and went out to pick up her prescriptions. The next few days, she settled back into life, not cooking much because of her hand, but he found he enjoyed cooking for her.

On Wednesday, he found her outside. "Hey, so how was today?"

She shrugged then turned to face him. It looked like she'd been crying, but he didn't want to make a big deal out of it.

"I don't want to be useless. I want to cook dinner for you, but I can't use my hand yet."

"It's okay. Is that the only reason you're upset?" He wanted to pry open her emotions and fix everything, but fixing it all for her was impossible. He had to allow her to get through the pain on her own with encouragement from him.

Candace shook her head. Her eyes closed, and a shudder ripped through her. Worry filled him. He dropped to one knee beside her.

"What's going on?"

"One of the guys who'd been taken prisoner with me died."

"Oh no, what happened?"

Adam struggled to remember the Marines who'd been with her. They'd been utterly unremarkable, maybe even sullen. Candace had stuck out, but those other guys blended into the background.

"Who was it?"

"Mike Kallas. It was a hit and run. He was on his motorcycle, and someone plowed into him. It was bad from what they said. No one got a good look at the driver."

"Wow." The hair on Adam's arms rose, and his neck tingled. Something was wrong. No one saw the driver. Had Kallas been targeted? He knew Candace had nothing to do with it. What if…no, he pushed the thought away. He wouldn't go into what-ifs, not now. He needed to take care of Candace and get her healthy.

"You know I like taking care of you. You're not a bother at all."

"You keep saying that, but I don't feel like I'm doing anything."

"Well, you're healing right now. I've spent my entire life not having anyone cook for me, and I enjoy doing things for you." His stomach twisted. He wasn't telling the whole truth. He had to tell. "So back in my twenties, I got married. She thought being with a Navy guy would make her special. Come inside, and I'll tell you the story while I cook us dinner."

Candace nodded, and he turned to step in before he paused and spun to her, pulling her into a hug that turned into a kiss. When he lifted his head, her eyes were shining with tears. He ran his thumb over her soft cheek, wiping away the moisture.

"It'll be okay," Adam said.

She nodded and gripped him tighter with her good hand. They stood together for a long minute. When she let go, he opened the door for her and then followed her inside.

He pulled chicken and peppers along with some broccoli from the refrigerator. As he grabbed a pot for rice, he had to wave Candace out of the kitchen.

"Have a seat and let me tell you the story. There's no room for the two of us in here, anyway."

Candace huffed out a breath, then turned to the table and pulled out a chair. "I wish I could help."

"I know, but right now, I'm taking care of you." He grabbed the rest of the ingredients he needed and started talking. "I was young, cocky as shit, and thought I would be something big because I planned to apply to be a SEAL. She wanted the fame of me being a SEAL, but she didn't realize being in the military isn't all fun and games. She got in a few bar fights, trashed some guy's condo, and ended up being arrested for drunk and disorderly while I was doing duty overseas. This was before I got my acceptance into BUD/s. When I received the news, it was one of the most heartbreaking and awakening moments of my life."

"That sounds terrible." Candace said nothing for a moment. "So how was it awakening?"

He finished cutting the chicken then tossed it in the pan to cook. "For some stupid reason, I believed giving her commands would make her do what I wanted. Like I said, I was young and stupid. I'd bought into the crap about the man being the head. From that experience, I realized you can't force someone into being what you want. You either are, or you aren't on the same page, fighting for the same thing. She didn't want the realities of being a Navy wife. I wasn't willing to give up the military. Divorce is no fun."

"I'm sorry."

"She married some guy in Florida. Last I heard they have a few kids and are happy. I don't wish her ill, I just wish I'd been more mature and been able to realize she wasn't the right woman for me. It almost wrecked my life."

Adam's lips turned down in a sad tilt. She hadn't ever met anyone she considered marriage material until Adam. She would be devastated if she'd found someone and then had to let them go because of their actions.

Maybe marriage wasn't in the cards for her. Lust still hit her at times, and she'd woken from erotic dreams, but the reality of being captured and raped meant her hang-ups prevented her from moving forward with sex even if she wanted to. It was a strange position to be in. She wanted Adam, but when she imagined him hanging above her with his dick about to enter her, she panicked. She never wanted to be vulnerable again.

"How did it almost wreck your life, other than the obvious of divorce?" Was her question too intrusive? "You don't have to answer."

"No, I will."

He stirred the chicken then started cooking the vegetables, his emotions playing across his face. It was one of the first times she'd seen him this open. Usually, there was a guarded stance he took. He might smile or laugh or grow serious, but he always kept a tight rein on his emotions. In this instance, he was open for her to read.

Adam drew in a deep breath before he started speaking. "Like I said, I wasn't acting smart in my twenties. I was angry about everything she had done so I went out one night, got drunk and did some stupid stuff. You know, started a fight, talked big, almost got busted by MPs. It was stupid, and I learned an important lesson."

She leaned in, drawn to him the more he talked. "What was the lesson?"

"To remain calm. I almost let something stupid like a woman dumping me ruin my chances of becoming a SEAL. I can't react. I know it's human nature to react, to get upset, but I have to stay calm. I garden. I run and exercise. I've learned how to channel my anger into something else. I don't want to spend my life being pissed something didn't happen the way I wanted. Sure, I'd love to find a place to live without the military telling me what to do and where to go, but this is my life. I enjoy being a SEAL. It takes sacrifices, and I'm willing to give up a few things to continue to be a Seal. And I like to cook, too."

Candace's eyebrows shot up. "You do?"

"Yeah, I do. It would be cool to take a cooking

class together. I've always wanted to do one of those weekends with a chef thing. They have them in places like Napa or Sedona. But most of those are for couples and it's weird going alone."

She warmed. That he wanted to do something like a cooking class with her was amazing. She'd never had anyone want to do something like that with her. In high school, she'd been awkward, and once she graduated, she went directly into the Marines. She had friends, and her best friend, Axel, had been special, but she'd never really had a good dating relationship as an adult.

"You're a complex man, Adam."

Her gaze warmed Adam. This woman made everything better. She may not know it, and she may not understand it, but she was perfect for him. If she hadn't been held captive, he probably would have convinced her to let him push her over the table so he could take her from behind. The reality was he had to go slow. She deserved more than some pseudo-porn proposition with wild meaningless sex because sex with Candace would never be meaningless.

He hadn't been called out on a mission since she'd come to stay with him, but the itchy feeling in his gut had started a few days ago and gotten worse when he found out the other guy they'd rescued with her had been killed.

When he had to leave town for a week or two, would she stick around and not make a mess of his life? Or would he come home to some sort of hell he would be forced to clean up?

# CHAPTER 9

Candace started back with counseling a week after her surgery. Being with Adam was pushing her to recover. She wanted things with Adam she couldn't get with anyone else. It wasn't just how hot he was, she liked spending time with him. He made her feel good about herself, which wasn't something any man before Adam had done. That he was a SEAL blew her mind. There were so many stories about SEALs being tough-as-nails hard-ass jerks, but Adam was a good guy.

Her hand was healing nicely though her activities were greatly restricted. Washing dishes was impossible, but minor cooking wasn't bad. Adam had brought home a steak for tonight's dinner.

Her phone rang, and she picked up the line, surprised Adam was calling her in the middle of the day.

"Hey, what's up? I'm a little shocked to get a call from you at this time," Candace said.

"We're on our way out of town," Adam said. "We're taking off in, well, a few seconds. I can't tell you where I'm headed or how long I'll be."

She stared at the refrigerator, not really seeing it. This is what it was like to be left behind.

"Candace, are you still there?"

She recovered quickly. "Yes. Sorry, I didn't mean to zone out. Um, okay. First, be safe, kick-ass, get the bad guys, and then come home."

His chuckle warmed her. She turned away from the refrigerator, wondering how she would get through the next few days or weeks being alone.

"I'll call you when I'm done," Adam said.

"Hey," Candace said.

"Yeah?"

Other people were speaking in the background and someone yelled. Maybe she shouldn't say anything, but she had to. This might be her last chance. "I care about you. I just wanted you to know. You matter to me."

The sound of him drawing in a sharp breath

made her stomach tingle. She'd surprised him or something. What she had wasn't love yet, but it was close.

"Thank you for saying that. I care about you, too." Neither said anything for a moment. "I'll be home soon. We're taking off. I've got to go."

Desperation made her throat clench. "I'll see you in a few."

"In a few."

The call ended. A huge hole opened in her chest, leaving her empty. She didn't want him to fly off to rescue other people. But this was what Adam did. He kept the world safe. She'd been in the same or similar position not too long ago. At one point, she'd been the one rescuing, and then she'd turned into the one who needed to be saved. No question, her next therapy session, she'd have to discuss her feelings.

The weekend dragged on with no doctor's appointments or therapy sessions. She headed to the zoo for the afternoon on Sunday, just trying to find something to pass the time. Once her appointments started up on Monday, the days went by faster. By Friday, when she hadn't heard from Adam, she started to worry.

Part of her recovery was not watching the news

and obsessing about where the US military was sending people. But with Adam out on a mission, she ached to know where he was and what he was doing. She had to convince herself he wouldn't get captured like she had. Her situation had been different. The reason they'd been caught was they hadn't been prepared for what they'd stumbled into. Adam and his team were trained to do exactly what they were on a mission for. They weren't jaded or lazy, just biding their time until their next post, they were SEALs out to take down the bad guy and save the day.

Therapy had taught Candace a lot about forgiveness. She'd had to forgive the men who had been goofing around with the snake, the people who had delayed them, the people serving with her who had failed on their mission, and herself. With Mike's death, she'd realized she hadn't forgiven them. It wasn't good for her to hold on to the hate and anger. She needed to let it all go.

There were times she berated herself for not pushing them to leave the area earlier, but she hadn't been the person in command, and the decision hadn't been hers. If she played through all likely scenarios, it would drive her crazy. She'd done everything to survive.

It was a little odd living in Adam's house without him there. She adapted to being alone but wished she had more friends close by. It sucked that all her close friends in the Marines were dead. She needed to find a new group of people she jelled with, but the older she got, the harder it became. She jelled with Adam and his team, but they were gone. One day, it would be nice to have a good group of friends, but she wasn't sure it would happen any time soon.

In the middle of the second week without Adam, she heard through the email loop Greg had been murdered. It was shocking because he'd been taken from his apartment and drug out to the middle of nowhere and shot. After she received the email from an acquaintance, she'd looked for information on the case. The police had no idea who had killed him, but they were looking for leads.

It was odd that two of the people who had been captured in Iraq and taken to Iran had died. She had thanked her lucky stars they'd survived, but to come back from being captured and be brutally murdered at home was awful.

* * *

Almost three weeks had gone by. Her hand was

better though she still couldn't use it, she at least could move a little, and the pain was less. She would have to train her fingers to do everything all over again. She'd gone to bed, making sure the doors and windows were locked. When a noise woke her, she almost jumped out of her skin. The sound was loud, like someone was inside the house. Panic filled her, and then the door to her bedroom opened. Fear whipped through her like a gunshot. Had someone come to murder her?

"It's me, Adam."

"Jesus," she whispered before turning on the lamp beside her bed. "You're home."

"Yeah. I showered at the base."

"Come here." Candace opened her arms and relief filled her when Adam came closer. He switched off the light, and she snuggled close, wrapping one leg over his.

Her skin tingled but being vulnerable with a guy killed all of her desire. She didn't pull away from Adam though she should. Sending mixed messages was wrong, but she couldn't ignore the desire to have him running through her. It did take a long time to fall asleep with him beside her.

Adam was glad to be home. He'd missed Candace. After the mission was complete, while they were still in Germany, he'd pined for Candace. The guys had joked about how whipped he was, and he nodded and chuckled with them.

Their mission had drained them all. It had been seven days in Turkey, getting little sleep as they tracked down and killed a band of rebels who were trying to disrupt the area. They'd kidnapped and tortured key Turkish political figures and their families, leaving the US military little wiggle room for capturing them and bringing them in. His team had killed stealthily, making it look like their own men had turned on each other.

When they finally took care of the last of the men, they'd found the daughters of a few politicians. Their families were gone, but the girls would survive. He and his team had taken them to a live-in school that would help them, not condemn them for whatever those assholes had done.

Archer drifted off but had a hard time staying asleep. Agitation ate at him, waking him for the day. After a quick stop by the bathroom he fixed a bowl with fruit, oats, and nuts mixed with yogurt then stumbled out to his back yard. Candace had done a great job taking care of his plants. He needed to do a little trimming, but they'd been watered. He'd come home a few times to dead flowers because he had no one to water them while he was gone. Usually, he would toss those into his compost box and head out to buy new flowers.

He wanted something yellow back here, so he headed out to a close market and picked up a few pots of daisies. Flowers made him remember there was more to life than what he did as a SEAL. There were happy people out there who lived beautiful lives without all the killing. Those were the people he battled for every day.

When Candace woke, he wasn't in bed. She sat up slowly and glanced around, wondering if she'd dreamed him up. No, his shirt was on the floor next to her bed. He'd been here. She used the bathroom before she searched him out. He was in the back yard, planting new flowers.

"Hey," she said as she stepped outside and set her coffee mug on the small table in the corner. She moved closer and kissed him on the cheek before returning to her coffee.

Adam finished with the flowers he was working on, then stood and came over to her. "Thank you for holding me when I got home."

"You're welcome." She took a sip of coffee and then met his gaze, seeing the haunted look. "Anything you can tell me?"

He shrugged. "It was rough."

"I'm sorry. I'm here for you. Even if it is just knowing I watered your plants."

His chuckle warmed her. "Thank you. I had to get new flowers, something yellow to brighten the area."

She surveyed his work. It did brighten the area. She liked the yellow flowers. They brought happiness to the back yard. "I like it."

"I'm headed over to the bar later to shoot the shit with the guys."

"I have therapy this afternoon. I'll be back later. If you want to eat here, just send me a text, and I'll make sure the food is warmed up."

He squeezed her shoulder. "You're too nice. Seriously, you're way too nice."

"Hey, I wasn't a SEAL, but I was a Marine. I know after a bad mission, the last thing you need is someone all over you. If you come home late and want to crawl into bed with me, I'm okay with that. I just..." She trailed off, unable to say the words.

"I won't push you on sex."

Her cheeks heated. "Thank you."

She wasn't sure she could ever have sex again. In her private sessions with the therapist, she'd gone into how much sex turned her off. She was working through the issue, but it was slow going. No question, Adam wouldn't wait forever. She eyed him, taking in his powerful muscles, his height, how sexy he looked, and knew if she didn't put out soon, another woman would.

# CHAPTER 10

Adam wanted to spend more time with Candace, but he was due back at the base this morning. He and his team had blown off steam, played volleyball, watched sports, and done all the things they needed to do to stay on the right side of sanity.

He wanted Candace but pushing her to have sex would only get her to leave. She had to come to him in her own time. For now, he would jack off in the shower. She didn't need him crawling all over her like some out-of-control dog.

The Thursday after they got back, they were called into a meeting about activity in the middle east. He wasn't thrilled the area they'd just come from was unstable again. If something didn't change soon, they would end up deployed for six months. It was the last thing he wanted. Their cycle shouldn't come up for another eighteen months, but when Uncle Sam sent them, they went.

Some days he felt like the world was on fire. Today was one of those days. He hated the way these idiots would go in to take over some area and try to kill as many innocents as possible. Killing people sucked, even when he did it. At least the kills he made were to stop other people from dying. He had a hard time reconciling deaths at first, but sometimes hard measures had to be taken to prevent even worse tragedies.

The door opened, and more people strolled in. It was Wolf and his team. They gave chin lifts all around as they took their seats. This meeting just turned interesting.

"Good afternoon, gentlemen and ladies," Dallas Creed, the commander of Bravo, said as he moved to the front of the room. "We're about to get into the details of our mission in just a moment. First, I wanted to assure all of you we aren't deploying overseas long-term."

"Well, thank goodness," Flip said.

"Shut it, Flip," Mist said. "I wanted to go and get more hazard pay. I found a new car."

"You and your cars. Just sell one of them, and then you'll have your hazard pay," Wolf countered.

"How many cars you have now?" Abe asked.

Mist crossed his arms over his chest and flashed them a smile. "Three."

"Okay, boys, time to get back on task," Creed said. "We're headed to Bosnia tomorrow morning."

A few people groaned. At least he wasn't leaving for six months.

"How long?" Sugar asked.

"Two weeks at least. Maybe three."

"Crap," Sugar said under his breath.

"I know you all have lives here," Creed said. "But this is what we signed up for. We'll be back in a few weeks and life will go on. Your wife and baby will be fine, Sugar."

Murmurs went around the room. The guys who had wives would have to say goodbye. For the rest of them, it was just getting life in order like paying bills. Of course, with Candace at his place, he didn't want to leave, but this was what being a SEAL was about. She wasn't his wife, but she was important in his life.

Creed continued talking and pointed to the screen showing a compound in the mountains. "This compound will host a set of meetings our primary target will attend." Creed moved to the corkboard and tacked a photo to the top in the center. "We will capture this man and get information from him. That is our primary objective. We have four other objectives, and we'll be working with Master Chief Steel. Wolf's team will take point on the operation under Commander Hurt's authority."

No one said anything as the severity of the mission sank in. They were sending two SEAL teams out. This was big. Wolf was someone Archer looked up to. The man had proven himself time and time again. He was glad they were working with Wolf and his team. The men were all at the top of their game. Adam appreciated his team and how well they worked, but he looked to Wolf for where they needed to be.

Their plane was taking off at four the next morning. He hated breaking the news to Candace, but at least he had the chance to say goodbye this time.

He pulled into his driveway and cut the engine to his truck. When he opened the door, Candace's voice drifted out through the open windows. He closed his eyes, listening to her sweet voice. It wove around him, making him hard. He wanted to pull her into his arms and make love to her all night long, but there was no way she would want sex yet.

"Oh hey, you're home early," Candace said as he stepped into the house.

"Yeah." He moved to her and pulled her into a hug. She melted against him, her body fitting against his perfectly. Candace was exactly the type of woman he wanted in his life.

She leaned back, and her eyebrows cocked up. Archer stepped closer and brushed his lips over hers. Her hand was on his back, and she kissed him like she meant it. He moaned as his tongue twisted with hers. They belonged together, no question.

His cock grew even harder as he held her. She tilted her head back and deepened the kiss. Her hand on his arm was driving him crazy. He picked her up and carried her to the couch, lowering her gently to the cushions. Lust pumped hot as he held himself up so he didn't crush her. If he had half a mind he would stop, but his hand was on her ribs, and her breasts were right there. The urge to strip her hit him like a rogue wave he had to force away. Maybe he stiffened first, but she clenched her muscles, making him draw away.

"I'm sorry. Too much too soon?"

Candace hid her face with her hand. Was she crying? He didn't want to touch her if she didn't want to be touched, but he needed to make sure she was okay. He stepped over to the couch and pulled her up, moving her to his lap.

"I'm sorry."

She shook her head against his chest. "No. It's not you, it's me."

She was right, it was her and telling her it wasn't wouldn't move them forward. She had to deal with everything in her head, and he wanted to give her time, but she was the person who had to move forward.

Panic filled Candace. She was fucking up and fucking with Adam's life. "I should leave." The words spilled out. She wanted to be with Adam, but she didn't know if a relationship was possible. Day after day, the memories haunted her. She wanted to get better, but she wasn't sure how. The guys who had abducted her had abused her terribly. In her heart, she knew Adam wasn't like them, but sex worried her, and he wanted sex.

If only she'd met him before she'd been taken. Or maybe if she hadn't been abducted and the men who had been clowning around had listened. Of course, then she never would have met Adam. It sucked that the best person she'd ever known came into her life when the worst thing had happened to her.

Her words cut him to the core. He didn't want

her to go. His need for her had grown. "Why would you leave?" God, he sounded pathetic.

"You aren't the type of man who can live without...without sex."

Her voice cut out as she spoke. He wanted to grab her shoulders and shake her. He needed her, not sex. "You don't know that." Anger tinged his voice. He could live without sex. He wasn't so basic he would put fucking above love.

She launched off his lap, her anger rising. He was lying to her, which was the last thing she needed. "Are you okay without having sex?" Her gaze drilled into his. She'd known plenty of men in the Marines who had wonderful women at home, and they would fuck around, having sex with awful women when deployed. They cheated on their wives and girlfriends like it was no big deal. Would he lie to her and say he wasn't cheating while he was going behind her back to fuck some skanky woman?

Adam blew out a breath as his cock deflated even more. The snarky reply on the tip of his tongue died. Spouting off wouldn't help.

"Please sit with me. We have something special. I want to talk this through, not fight."

Her lips thinned, and her eyes narrowed before

she closed her eyes and a single tear traced down her cheek. "But I'm broken."

He reached for her and pulled her to the couch beside him. His heart went out to her. She was trying to be brave and trying to spare them both some pain. Sex had been an important part of his life for the last few years. Being a SEAL meant he didn't have to search for sex. Women threw themselves at him and his teammates, offering pussy like free candy. But Archer wanted a partner who made him laugh. Explaining his desire and needs to Candace might take more time than he had. He was leaving in the morning, and he didn't want her to doubt his feelings.

"Darling, we're all a little broken. I need help, too. There are times I have to shove that shit deep and keep pressing on. The only reason I'm not on the floor dying is because the stuff I deal with doesn't happen to me personally." He turned to face her and cupped her cheeks. "You went through so much. You survived, and you're getting stronger. I can wait."

She searched his eyes, looking for the lie or some deception. There was none. He was being truthful. Still, she needed to make sure he understood it may not ever happen. She needed more therapy. Maybe she should give in and let him have sex. Her stomach cramped and her lungs squeezed. She couldn't allow anyone to dominate her.

Would he wait? She didn't want to have her heart broken because she'd trusted the wrong person. Already her heart was on the edge of reason. She had fallen for Adam but held back in telling him. She wanted their life to be good together. What if he had sex with someone else? It would be okay, she guessed, as long as he came home to her.

Her stomach rolled. No way could she deal with that. Her life was so messed up. The group of terrorists had tried to ruin everything for her. They were winning. There were only two of them left from the ambush. Sure, Mike and Greg had died over here under weird circumstances, but the rest had been taken out by the terrorists. She wanted to win, to overcome whatever was wrong in her life, but so much still held her back.

"Candace, I'll wait however long you need."

He would wait for a long time for sex with Candace because she was different. She wasn't the type of woman you fucked and forgot. Candace would stay with him forever. She was the woman he wanted for a wife. Sure, they had a lot to overcome, but he was willing to be with her even if it meant sex took a while to get to.

"I have to be at the base at three-thirty tomorrow morning." He wanted his goodbye to be happy, Mostly, he didn't want to have to worry about her taking off. "We'll be gone for at least two weeks."

Candace frowned. "Oh."

"I want you to understand how much you mean to me. Yes, if you're willing to have sex, then I want the same, but I won't pressure you into having sex. We have time. We have loads of time."

Candace blew out a shaky breath. "I'll stay. But once you're home, you need to come to therapy with me."

His heart rate picked up. They would find some way to move forward with their relationship. He was grateful she'd suggested it. If she wanted him at therapy, then the chance was good that she wouldn't leave while he was gone.

"Yes. I'll be there. It'll be good to talk everything out."

She nodded, then stood. He hopped up and reached for her, pulling her into a hug. He kept his touch as platonic as possible, breathing in her scent as he tried to soak in the feel of her. Being gone for two weeks would be difficult. But knowing Candace would be here when he returned would make the time away worth it.

# CHAPTER 11

Archer signaled to Wolf they were ready. He inched into position, his scope sighted on the man standing in the front yard of the compound they'd surrounded.

"Bravo One to Alpha One, we're in position."

"Alpha One to Alpha Two, it's a go."

Archer watched through the scope, making sure the guy he had his rifle trained on didn't budge while Abe, Cookie, and Mozart advanced into the house from the back. Archer's team was providing cover for the men who were breaching the building. The compound they were attacking had advanced security for most places in this area of the world, and the last thing any of them wanted was for Wolf's team to be trapped in the compound with no way out.

They'd been in Bosnia for nine days. Once they apprehended the subject, they would head to Italy for a few days then back to the USA. He wanted to speak to Candace and find out how she was doing, but they'd been on since the moment they arrived and didn't have a chance to chat with anyone at home.

Sugar had to feel the pinch. The man's kid would be born soon, and Sugar wasn't home to see the birth. Archer knew it was killing Sugar, but he wasn't allowing it to affect his work.

Something inside the compound exploded. Archer didn't hesitate and took out the man he had his rifle on. The guy dropped hard. Archer glanced around, seeing four other men in the dirt. His men had done exactly what they'd been trained to do.

"Alpha One, state your position." Archer waited, praying the men hadn't been harmed. Losing Wolf and his team would devastate the SEAL community. The seconds ticked by, and Archer's anger increased.

"Alpha team has the package in tow." The words from Wolf brought relief. "We have one team member who rung his bell. We're coming out."

Archer watched as Alpha team exited the building. A noise sounded behind Archer. He turned over just as something landed heavy where he'd been. He fired off a shot, his heart racing as he gasped.

"Watch your six, Bravo. We've got tangos in the wind." Archer scrambled up and searched the area, looking for any more movement. His body was on high alert. Someone had tried to end him. If he hadn't been paying attention, he would be dead.

*Shit, that was close.*

Candace would be pissed if he didn't come home. Had he been distracted? No, he hadn't. The attacker had just been silent. Next time, he would add in one more check to make sure they didn't have anyone sneaking up on him.

Archer moved to the rendezvous point, forcing his body and mind to calm. They met up with Alpha team and made their way to the other side of the hill where a helicopter was supposed to pick them up at two in the morning. The area was dark, and the sky was full of stars. He missed home, missed his house, but most of all, he missed Candace. She was the reason to wake up in the morning and keep the world safe. Before Candace, he'd wanted to keep people safe on a broad level, but now, he wanted Candace's life to be good.

His team looked stressed, but so did Wolf's team.

This was supposed to be a simple catch and take, but they'd run into surprise after surprise.

"Call for exfil, Dude," Wolf barked.

"What happened in there?" Archer asked him.

"They blew themselves up rather than face capture. We got the man we wanted, but we almost were toast."

Archer looked over Wolf's team, noting how Benny was lying on the ground, his eyes closed. "That sucks. Is Benny okay?"

Wolf glanced over his shoulder. "Yeah, he'll be good. Needs to take it easy for a few weeks. He was hit hard." Wolf moved to talk to Abe.

Archer watched them interact. They were a lot like he and Flip. Archer's team members were his best friends now. How had Candace dealt with losing her best friends?

The helicopter arrived, and they loaded on, Archer sitting next to Flip. He leaned against his buddy, getting a little rest on their way back to base. They'd grabbed the guy who had information the military and CIA needed. He had fulfilled his part for this mission and now it was time to relax until the next one. He still loved his job, but he was thrilled they were headed home. When he arrived, he would make sure Candace knew he loved her no matter what. They would work through the sex thing.

"What happened out there?" Flip asked him.

The other guys were listening, but he didn't mind them hearing. When they unpacked the mission, they would go through it all. "I heard a noise behind me and turned over. Some guy threw a knife. It almost got me. I killed him."

"Glad you got him," Flip said. "It would have sucked to have to go to your funeral."

The guys all laughed and he joined in. It would have sucked for them and for Candace. Hell, it would suck going to any of their funerals. Somewhere in the mix, something had gone wrong. Once they figured out where the guy had come from, they'd know how they'd screwed up.

They landed in Italy, exhausted from their mission. Archer showered before finding a bunk. He'd found enough sleep to be deep in it when someone pounded on the door to the room where he had crashed.

"What is it?" He called out, angry to be disturbed.

"Master Chief Culver, you're needed now by Vice Admiral Beckett."

"Yes, sir." Archer sat up and wiped his face. He grabbed his toiletries bag and brushed his teeth, thankful he was a SEAL and had an excuse for not shaving. After swiping on some deodorant and splashing water on his face and hair, he grabbed clothes and was ready to race out the door in less than two minutes.

What the hell had happened that a Vice Admiral needed him? He hadn't ever been called into a Vice Admiral's office alone in his Navy career. If he received medals, it was a planned group activity. Getting called into the office was less than desirable.

When he opened the door to his room, an ensign stood in the hall, waiting for him. Archer saluted, and the ensign returned the gesture. "I'm to take you to Vice Admiral Beckett right now."

"Okay, ma'am, what's your name?" Archer wanted some coffee, maybe a little food, but Vice Admirals didn't wait for master chiefs, even if they were SEALs.

"I'm Ensign Calme," she said as she hurried along.

"Thank you for finding me."

"Yes, sir. It's just this way." The ensign turned down another hall.

The young ensign led Archer to the offices where he was escorted into a conference room. He thanked Ensign Calme and saluted the vice admiral.

"Master Chief Culver, sir."

"Yes. At ease. There's been an issue back home. We wanted you to tell your man."

A cold chill raced through Archer as dread settled on him. He already hated what Beckett had to say, and he hadn't even heard it.

"First Class Washington's wife went into labor. Something went wrong."

Archer drew in a quick breath, praying he didn't fall over. Fuck, Sugar would be devastated.

"By the time she made it to the hospital, the baby was already gone," Beckett said. "She didn't make it."

Tears filled his eyes as emotions rolled through him. He had to grab onto the chair he was standing behind so he didn't drop to the floor. He squeezed his eyes shut, trying not to cry in front of the vice admiral but failing miserably.

"Th—" his voice cut out as his throat closed. He had to swallow just to speak. "They both died, sir?"

"Yes, Master Chief Culver. I'm sorry for your team members. Washington is still asleep. We have a plane ready for your team to go. I know you were supposed to stay here until tomorrow when you left with Master Chief Steel's team, but we have a crew headed to DC. You'll pick up a plane in DC and get back to California tonight."

"Thank you, sir. How long until the flight?"

"Two hours."

Archer took the napkin offered by Beckett and wiped his eyes. He hadn't cried this much in years. Maybe since one of his buddies had passed away. He certainly hadn't shed any tears when his father died, and he'd never cried in front of an officer.

Beckett put his arm around Archer and gave him a quick hug. "We're very sorry over here. If there is anything..."

Archer nodded, but his words froze in his throat. Molly passing away was awful. The baby, heart wrenching. Archer's heart twisted uncomfortably. He hated the injustice of it all. He would gladly have died today if it meant Sugar had his wife and child. But that wasn't how tradeoffs worked.

Archer found the rest of the guys, telling them they were flying out in under two hours. A few of the men complained, but when they saw his hard expression, they changed their tune.

"What's up, boss?" Flip asked.

"Bad shit all around. We're headed out to hangar one. I have to talk to Sugar." The words were spat out with anger and pain.

Flip shot him a weird glance then gave him a quick nod. "I'll make sure everyone gets to hangar one right now."

"Thank you." Archer pulled Flip into a hug, squeezing tight, hoping a bit of Flip's bravery rubbed off on him. "When you're done, come get Sugar's stuff."

"Shit," Flip spit out but said nothing else.

He hadn't told Flip, but the man knew it was bad if Archer was telling him to get Sugar's gear. Archer knocked on the door where Sugar was sleeping. He knocked again, pounding hard.

"What?" Sugar yelled.

"Open up. It's Archer. I need to talk to you."

"Yes, sir." The door opened, revealing Sugar in nothing but underwear. "This had better be good, sir."

"Get your clothes on." If Archer showed any emotions now, he'd never get Sugar dressed.

Sugar turned and pulled on his pants then his shirt. "Can I piss and brush my teeth?"

"Yes." He wanted to say more, to be kinder, but he was dying inside. Any show of compassion would cue Sugar into the fact something was wrong. They needed to be out of this small room and in the open. Sugar was going to explode.

Sugar didn't bother to shut the door. They'd seen each other naked and had to take dumps in front of each other on more than one occasion while on missions. Sugar was his brother, and nothing would take that away. This would hurt the entire group. They'd lose hope, maybe be called off for a few missions, he wasn't sure. This kind of loss rocked people to the core, and they needed everyone at one hundred percent. But life took things none of them wanted to give.

"You going to tell me what the hell is going on?" Sugar asked.

"Hangar one." He led Sugar outside and was halfway to the hangar when Sugar put his hand on Archer's arm.

Archer stopped and turned to face him. He blew out a breath, pain filling every cell of his body. This was the hardest thing he'd done in his life. BUD/s wasn't even this difficult. Maybe because there was an ending to BUD/s, but there wasn't any ending to this. Archer ached for this man. He wished he had Candace here to hold him.

"Fuck, Archer. What the hell is going on?" Sugar demanded.

"This morning, Molly went into labor." Archer saw the spark of excitement before it quickly diminished as Sugar took in Archer's serious expression. There was no way to ease into this. "There was an issue."

"No. No," Sugar said as he clutched Archer's arm.

"The baby was already gone by the time she made it to the hospital. Molly didn't—"

"Fuck!" Sugar roared. He turned and found a light pole, slamming his fist into the metal time and time again.

The guys from their team ran over, but there was nothing they could do to stop Sugar. Archer and the rest of the men stood back, protecting Sugar from everyone around them as he found a tree and pulled down a branch, breaking it in two, then breaking the branch again. He yelled and screamed his rage, looking like a beast.

When the MPs showed up, Archer stopped them, telling the guys Sugar had just lost his wife and baby in birth. The men stood back, giving Sugar space.

When his buddy finally dropped to the ground and pounded his fists, screaming Molly's name, the rest of the SEAL team moved in, holding their brother as he shouted curse words. Medical personnel arrived, but Sugar refused drugs to dull the pain. He would behave on the aircraft.

Archer already saw the numbness settling in. He, along with help from his team, pulled Sugar up and helped him toward the plane.

"Master Chief Culver," someone called from

behind him. He stopped walking and turned. It was Ensign Calme from earlier. "Master Chief Culver, sir, Vice Admiral Beckett sent me. I have something."

Agitation filled Archer. He needed to get Sugar into his seat. "Spit it out, Ensign."

"The baby didn't die. There was a mistake in communicating. Vice Admiral Beckett called the hospital to see if he could do anything. He has a picture." Ensign Calme held up her phone.

Sugar whipped around, tears still streaming as he grabbed the phone and stared at the screen. His shoulders shook as more tears flowed.

Sugar glanced up, pinning the ensign with a hard stare. "Are you sure?"

"Yes, sir. I was in the room when Vice Admiral Beckett called. I heard the conversation. I'm sorry about your wife, but the baby survived. She's perfect and healthy."

There wasn't a dry eye amongst them. Even the MPs were openly crying. Sugar had received the worst and the best news of his life. He handed the phone back to Ensign Calme and turned to the plane.

"Give me your phone number, and I'll text the photo to you," Ensign Calme said.

Archer held out his hand and took her phone,

texting the photo to himself. "Thank you, Ensign Calme."

"You're welcome, and I'm glad there was something good. Take care and be safe."

He nodded before he turned to his team, watching as they helped Sugar into the plane. Sugar's world had been destroyed, but he had some small hope. The flight took too much time, and though they all slept, when they arrived in California, Archer felt like he'd been run through BUD/s hell week again and punched in the gut for his effort.

He drove Sugar to the hospital. They were given security passes to get into the nursery. He stepped into the hall with the windows showing all the babies, and his heart nearly shattered at the sight.

Candace was sitting in a rocking chair, bottle in one hand, the baby cradled in her arm. By the way her mouth was moving, she was singing. He melted. All of his SEAL badassness went out the window, and he was at her mercy.

Sugar's hand clamped around his forearm. "Oh God, Archer. What if I can't do this?"

Archer grabbed Sugar's hand and squeezed. "Dion, you'll be a great dad. We'll figure out the details later. You care, and your being there more than anything will make a difference. You'll be a wonderful father."

A nurse stepped out and smiled. "Let me introduce you to your baby. We've been calling her darling because we didn't know what you wanted to name her."

"Ella," Dion said. "Short for Elizabeth. It's what Molly wanted."

"Ella is beautiful. Candace has been here since the beginning other than to shower and sleep for a few hours here and there."

Sugar nodded and moved into the nursery. Archer hung back, feeling way too huge to be so close to such a tiny thing. Candace put the bottle down and adjusted, getting a good hold on the baby before she stood. Sugar settled in the rocking chair, worry creasing his brows. His hands shook, and fear flashed over his features. Archer hadn't ever seen Sugar look scared of anything, and the man had gone up against cold-hearted killers, but his tiny Ella scared the crap out of him. Archer knew if the positions were reversed, he'd be terrified he would fuck up.

Candace handed the baby to Sugar. It took a moment for him to relax enough to settle back against the chair. The baby squawked but settled after a moment. Candace gave Sugar the bottle she'd been using. The nurse helped him position the baby and started offering other instructions.

Candace stepped away, her smile watery as she left the nursery and headed to him. He opened his arms and wrapped her in a hug. If he'd had doubts earlier, he didn't now. He was in love. Candace had taken care of his brother's child while they'd been away on a mission. She didn't have to. She wasn't close with Molly as far as he knew, and she didn't owe Dion anything.

"Thank you," Archer choked out.

Candace's smile brightened his day. She was the best thing to come home to. "She's beautiful."

"You've been there the whole time?"

"Almost. I took a short break, but otherwise, I've been right here."

He had so many questions, but those could wait. Sugar looked up at them, his eyes full of wonder. He mouthed thank you to Candace, and she moved to him. Archer followed and stared down into the sweet but scrunched-up face of Ella.

"She's beautiful," Archer said.

"She is," Sugar whispered. "I've never felt like this in my entire life. I don't know what this is."

"Pure love," Archer said.

Sugar went back to staring at Ella, his large hands seeming to dwarf the baby. He and Candace left the nursery but waited for Sugar to step out once the baby was sleeping.

Archer went to him and wrapped his arms around his buddy. The grief came out in a shuddering breath that expressed all the anger and sadness wrapped up inside.

"I need to call people," Sugar said.

"Molly's mother is on her way," Candace offered. "She's coming from New York. Wanted to drive out."

"Okay." Sugar frowned.

"She doesn't have to be here," Archer said.

"It's her mother." Sugar let out a harsh sigh. "The woman hates me, but it's her mom."

"Why?" Candace asked.

Sugar hit Candace with a sharp look. "I'm black, and Molly wasn't. It was enough for her mother to be pissed about."

Archer reached out and squeezed Sugar's arm. "We've got your back."

"Speaking of that." Sugar placed his hand on Candace's shoulder. "I can't thank you enough for staying with my daughter."

Candace shook her head. "I was happy to." She'd

been worried when Molly had called her and said something was wrong. She'd walked her through getting an ambulance, but Molly had passed out before Candace arrived. Tears gathered in her eyes, and she had to blink them back. "Later, after you settle, I'll tell you everything. I wanted to help. You're Archer's family." She squeezed Dion's arm. "I've got group therapy twice a week. Otherwise, I have little going on."

Dion nodded. "I don't know what to do."

Candace had doctor's appointments but that was it. "Well, first off, I'll be there."

"And we'll make sure you get the leave you need to sort through things," Archer said.

Dion sighed. "Is it bad I would rather do another mission than have to fix this stuff here?"

Archer chuckled. "No, buddy, it's not bad."

"I just don't know…" Dion turned to stare into the nursery at his sleeping child.

"Hey," Candace said, her emotions riding high. She'd had time to stuff down her sadness at seeing Molly's last minutes, but this brought them all back. She blew out a breath and put her arm around him. "I'm here to help. I'm serious. We'll help you through these first few months, and then everything will look better."

Candace offered so much support to Sugar, amazing Archer.

"You still have to arrange for a funeral. This is stressful. We'll help you get through this."

Sugar closed his eyes and shook his head. "God, this is going to suck."

Candace hugged Sugar again and then stepped away. Archer wrapped his arms around Sugar, holding him close. "We'll help."

"I'm sticking around to help with Ella," Candace said.

Sugar's shoulders shook as he nodded. "Thank you." Sugar blew out a breath, looking lost. "Thank you both."

The guys would help some, but Sugar was right, this would be hell to sort through. Who would take care of Ella if they went on a mission? He didn't want to lose Sugar, but the man may have to leave the military to take care of his family. It was selfish for Archer to want Sugar to stay with them, but he wasn't sure what other options there were for a single dad who was a SEAL. Sugar's life was forever changed by one tragedy and a miracle.

Archer glanced at Candace. If he was in Sugar's situation, he wasn't sure what he would do. Losing Candace would cut like a knife to his heart but having a part of her like Sugar had a part of Molly in Ella would be both wonderful and devastating. Archer wasn't sure he was strong enough to handle what Sugar would go through. Archer knew his weaknesses and had no doubt he would fold.

# CHAPTER 12

The next week was a swirl of crazy emotions and even more crazy events as Archer tried to help Sugar. The man was on leave for a few weeks, which Archer appreciated. No one at the base wanted Sugar to suffer.

Archer and Candace stayed at Sugar's house each night until Molly's mother, Norma, showed up. She demanded Sugar allow her to stay in the guest room, which meant he and Candace were back at his place.

Archer didn't like the way Norma acted toward Sugar. The man was kind, and that woman was treating Sugar like the devil. At least Candace was able to go over in the mornings and help with the baby.

The flowers needed watering and weeds needed

to be pulled, but flowers and weeds were the least of his worries. Work was a particularly lousy bag of dicks. Without Sugar there, everything was off. Emotions were running high. Flip blew up at Mist for nothing at all. Archer had to bring down the hammer, pissing off two friends at the same time.

There were times he wished he hadn't received the promotion to Master Chief. Black may outrank him since he was an officer, but on the team, Archer was in charge. There were times he wanted to hand over the command to Black, but the man was only a few months out of BUD/s and needed guidance. It was up to Archer to lead, even if he wanted to tell them all to fuck off. His team was family, and he didn't want any of them to leave, but he had so much anger from what had happened to Sugar.

The funeral for Molly was held the Thursday after her death. The naval base didn't shut down, but only a skeleton crew stayed behind. Tears were shed as they laid Molly to rest.

That weekend Archer headed over to Sugar's house early. Candace had a group session at eight but was planning on coming over immediately after. He was halfway up the walkway when he heard yelling. It wasn't Sugar. Instead, it was a woman. The low rumble of Sugar's voice filtered outside and was followed by more screeching.

Archer rang the bell, wondering what type of hell he was stepping into. The door opened, but Molly's mom blocked his entry.

"We're having a discussion. It's family only," the woman said before she tried to close the door.

Sugar came around the corner. "Oh no you don't. That's Archer, and he's welcome in my house all hours of the day or night. You remember Molly's mom, Norma." Sugar had the baby cradled in one arm while he carried around a blanket in the other.

Norma huffed. "It's Mrs. Devlin to you." She stomped off, following Sugar. "Give me the baby."

"No," Sugar said.

Archer imagined that if Sugar wasn't so big, this woman would tackle Sugar and take the baby. Sugar moved deeper into the house, and Norma followed.

"You can't keep her from me. I'll get custody. It would be easier if you just handed her over. Then we wouldn't have to go to court."

"No." Sugar didn't raise his voice, instead it was ice cold. "This is my baby. I'm not handing her over to you or anyone else."

"You can't take care of her!" Norma yelled.

Sugar didn't change his expression as he stared at

the woman. Archer looked from Norma to Sugar then back to her. She was being a bitch. Thankfully Ella slept through it all.

"What's going on?" Archer asked as he headed into the kitchen to wash dishes. Norma had come to help, but the place looked in total disarray. He and Candace needed to be here at night to help based on how dirty the countertops were. There was half heated food in the microwave and two pieces of toast in the cold toaster. Had Sugar even eaten this morning?

"I woke up to her packing Ella's things into her car. She already had Ella in the car seat and was trying to leave before I woke."

The words were a shock. "Excuse me?" Archer stared at his buddy, praying Sugar was exaggerating.

"I should have called the cops. Now, I've asked her to leave twice. I'm ready to call the cops if she doesn't get the hell out and leave me alone."

"You'll regret this," Norma said as she stalked over to the guest room grumbling the whole way.

"You need anyone else here?" Archer asked.

"Not sure." Sugar opened his refrigerator and stared inside, his face a mix of emotions. He closed the door, not getting anything out.

Archer stepped over and placed his hand on Sugar's shoulder. "Let me help you."

"I haven't even had any coffee, man. I woke up to find her taking my baby." Sugar's voice shook. He'd never seen his buddy this much of a wreck. "I'm so angry. If I didn't have Ella here, I might just kill her."

"Don't do that," Archer said. "Let her go."

"I'm scared she'll take the baby while I sleep."

Archer turned to look down the hall and make sure Norma wasn't headed their way. "You can stay at my place."

"What about Candace? Isn't she in your guest room?"

Archer warmed as he rubbed the back of his neck. "I kind of have been sleeping in the same room as her."

"Really? That's awesome." Sugar's smile stretched wide.

"What's awesome?" Norma was back, her lips turned down in a frown.

Archer cursed under his breath. He'd lost focus thinking about Candace. He needed to protect his buddy from the enemy, and right now, the enemy was Norma.

Since he didn't want to engage her in any serious discussion, he said nothing about Sugar coming to his house to stay. Instead, he started fixing Sugar breakfast. The woman needed to leave sooner rather than later.

"You need to go," Sugar said.

Norma huffed. "I'm not leaving without my baby."

Frustration built in Sugar's gaze. Archer needed to head this off, but Norma wasn't backing down, and Sugar wasn't giving in.

"She's not your baby," Sugar shot back.

Norma looked like she was gearing up to respond when Archer spoke.

"Get out." Archer didn't yell. Instead, he'd said the words with an icy calm that would chill anyone with half a brain. Norma didn't budge.

"You can't intimidate me away. I'm staying right here until you give me my baby."

Archer had had enough. If they were on base, the MPs would escort Norma away, but with the lack of housing on base, their team had been allowed to move to the city. Now he wished they had a larger piece of land for on-base housing.

He pulled out his phone and dialed the emergency number. Norma frowned at him, but it didn't stop him.

"What are you doing?" Norma quipped in her

shrill voice. She was getting on Archer's nerves. He had no clue how Sugar had put up with her.

"What Sugar should have done when he woke." The person on the other end of the line started talking, so Archer tuned into them. He gave the address and asked for an officer to stop by, giving brief details of what had happened.

"There's a patrol unit in your neighborhood. Someone should be there soon."

"Thank you." He hung up and met Norma's furious gaze. "Now, we wait."

Norma lifted her hand and shook her finger in Archer's face. "I'm calling my lawyer."

It took every ounce of self-control for Archer to stay calm. "Good, he can get you bail money." Archer shouldn't have added the last bit, but he was pissed. He didn't hit women, but he considered it since Norma was still trying to take Sugar's baby.

A car stopped outside, and Archer moved to the door, pulling it open. He stepped out and made sure the cops knew he wasn't armed.

"Sir, what seems to be the problem?" one of the officers asked.

"They've taken my baby and won't give it back," Norma wailed as she stepped outside and dropped to her knees. "I'm just a helpless woman, and they've taken my baby."

"Jesus," Archer said under his breath. "It's not your baby," he spoke loud enough for the cop to hear. "Your daughter gave birth and passed away. It's terrible, but she's not your baby."

"He wasn't there for the birth," Norma spit out as she stood, the tears she'd shed a few seconds ago had dried fast, and now she was back to shaking her finger at Archer. "He doesn't care about my daughter or my granddaughter. I'm getting custody, and he'll never see her."

Archer lifted his eyebrows before he met the officer's gaze. "She isn't telling the whole truth. My buddy, Dion Washington, is in the kitchen with his daughter. He woke up to find her packing the baby and the baby's things into her car. Dion didn't want cops involved because thought he could handle this. I showed up ten minutes later, and it was obvious she was still having issues. I called you guys when she threatened to take the baby again."

The officer turned from Archer to Norma. "Is that true?"

"She's mine. He can't take care of her. I'm taking her home where she'll be loved. He's a killer and can't be trusted."

The officer glanced at his partner as they slid their hands to their weapons. Archer imagined this situation turning rotten fast.

"Jesus, we're Navy SEALs, not murderers." Archer turned to the cops and hoped to get through them. "Please, don't believe a word she is saying. The baby will be taken care of. Sugar—Dion is a good man. He's a Navy SEAL, and he's big, but he's good."

The cop blinked at Archer twice before he lifted his brows. "So you're military, right?"

"Yes, sir. Navy, like I said."

"Call your people. We need to get this sorted." The officer moved to Norma and started talking.

Archer caught the officer's words. He was reading Norma the Miranda warnings. Archer almost laughed but decided it would be wrong to laugh at Norma being arrested. He wandered into the house as he called Dallas Creed.

"Hey, Archer, what's up?" Creed asked when he answered.

"Lieutenant, we've got a situation. Molly's mother tried to take Sugar's baby this morning."

"Fucking hell. You're kidding me, right?"

"I wish I was. I have the police here. Sugar is handling things well, but he could break at any moment. The cops asked for you to get involved."

"Shit. There goes my Saturday."

"Sorry, Creed. We could have—"

A door slammed, then Creed chuckled. "Sorry, my in-laws are here. I was acting for them. No bother, really. I'll be by in a moment. You're at Sugar's house?"

"Yes, sir."

"Give me twenty minutes."

"Sure thing. And thank you, sir."

Archer hung up and went to find Sugar again. One cop had Norma outside, talking to her about her options. Basically, he told her she might go to lockup if she didn't go home and forget this notion she had a right to the baby. Archer still planned on having Sugar and the baby sleep at his house. Sugar wouldn't be able to take losing Ella. It would be difficult for him to raise this baby, but SEALs stuck together, and he and his team would help Sugar.

Candace arrived before the cops left with Norma. They didn't take her in for suspected kidnapping. Instead, she kicked and punched one of the officers.

"Wow, totally crazy," Candace said as she settled in the rocking chair Sugar bought. Ella looked happy to be in her arms.

"Man, I have to thank you." Sugar was up pacing

the den. Creed had taken off, but the rest of the team was on their way over.

"Hey, guys, how about you two go work out? I'll take the baby to Adam's place, and we can chill there. Then this evening, you all can cook on the grill."

Sugar's lips turned down. "I don't know."

"I want to help, and you've got all this extra energy. If you wear yourself out, you'll feel better," Candace said. "Besides, Norma is out of the picture for a few hours. No way will she get bonded out before this evening, and she doesn't know where Adam lives."

"She's smart," Sugar said.

Candace positioned Ella to feed her. She had to watch her hand, but with the surgery she'd had, she could use her fingers now to brace the bottle. It took a little time to position the baby how she needed her, but she had no real problems holding Ella or feeding her.

The front door opened, and the guys came streaming in. For a group of large SEALs, they were nearly silent. She'd always thought big tough men were loud and annoying, but this group of guys adapted to the situation beautifully. She hadn't known them for long, but she liked Adam's team. The guys impressed her with their intense caring. All of them were taking Dion's loss hard, and all of them were sticking by his side. They had his back, even when Norma told them to leave, they still did little things for Dion and Ella. If only they'd all known how demented Norma was. With her gone, they could help again.

"How's the baby?" Flip asked.

"Good," Sugar said as he moved closer to Candace.

"Are you sure?" Flip asked.

Adam rolled his eyes. "Just look at her. She's happy."

"I need a ride over to Adam's place," Candace said.

Dion shook his head. "You've gotta start calling him Archer. That's what we call him."

She chuckled. "I like his name. Besides, I'm not you all. But I'll think about calling him Archer."

"Good." Dion bent over the baby and kissed her head. "He's a good man," Dion said so low Adam couldn't hear.

She chuckled and met Adam's gaze. "He sure is."

Archer warmed as he watched Candace with the baby. He'd known he'd found gold when he'd found her. She was taking care of his buddy's kid and sending them off to play. Few women would be so selfless. Later, he would surprise her.

"So, what are we doing?" Black asked.

"Sugar needs to work out. We'll tell you everything once we get to the base."

The guys jumped into action, packing everything Candace would need from formula to bottles and diapers with additional clothes for Ella. She asked them to include two baby blankets, and then she said she was set.

The guys piled into two trucks, dropping Candace off at Adam's place and making sure she was set before they headed to base. He loved coming onto base and kind of wished he still lived on base, but the housing shortage a few years ago had changed everything. Now with Candace in his life, he was happy he had a place to live together.

They piled out of the trucks, and Black led them in a short stretching session before they took off at a slow jog, making the loop around the base.

"What happened?" Flip asked.

Sugar explained with Archer interjecting what he observed when he arrived. The guys were pissed about what Norma had done. After their run, they jumped into the O course and pushed hard. It had been three hours of them talking and helping Sugar get his head on straight before they headed in to take showers. Wolf's team showed up and started shooting the shit.

"What's going on?" Wolf asked.

Archer glanced at Sugar, then spilled. "Archer's evil mother-in-law tried to kidnap the baby this morning. We came here to do some intense therapy."

"Well fuck," Wolf cursed.

"That's just wrong," Abe wrapped his arm over Sugar's shoulder and pulled him close. "Dude, we've all got your back."

The rest of the guys agreed, they had Sugar's back. Wolf pulled out his phone and started dialing.

"What are you doing?" Sugar asked.

"We'll pick up the slack and have a plan to make sure you have childcare. We have enough SEALs and retired SEALs in the area to cover you for a long while. Trust me, we'll help you."

"Really?" Sugar blinked at Wolf, and then a smile spread across his face.

"Yes," Wolf said. "Family takes care of family."

Archer and the guys showered, then Wolf found them while they were dressing.

"Caroline is organizing a calendar where people will put their availability. They've done this before when people get sick. She said she'll get with

Candace and help. Are you staying at Archer's house?"

"Yes, until we know Norma is gone or at least in jail."

"Good. Caroline and her friends are good at this."

"Wolf, we can't thank you enough," Archer said.

"I know you all would do the same for us." Wolf pulled Sugar in for a hug. Sugar pounded him on his back before letting go. Wolf stepped back and turned to Archer. "Anything comes up, you let me know."

"Sure thing, Chief."

Archer thanked his lucky stars Wolf knew what to do, and everything wouldn't fall to Candace. The baby, her care, all of it was overwhelming. As a SEAL, they relied on each other. His crew didn't have wives or serious girlfriends yet. Wolf and his team were lucky. Archer hoped his guys could be half as blessed. The SEALs would take care of Sugar and his family. No question, this group of men were the best people he'd ever known. Archer just hoped a judge would agree their solution for this situation was positive and never side with Norma in taking the baby away.

# CHAPTER 13

Candace was at therapy, and Cheyenne had the baby. They'd been going strong for two months. Sugar had gone back to work, and they were getting a guardianship set up so Candace would have custody of Ella when Sugar had to leave. It was scary, but after she'd arranged everything with the wives and girlfriends and a few giving and brave SEALs, she had confidence this would work. She and Adam would be guardians. For now, she was Ella's caregiver while Sugar worked. She had help with grocery shopping, they were giving her breaks, and she had support.

This was the first time since Axel had passed away she'd experienced being a part of a group.

Being with Adam was great, but she still didn't know where they were in their relationship.

"So, have you had sex yet?" The therapist's question seemed innocent enough, but it made her stomach cramp.

They hadn't had sex, and she knew Adam was getting frustrated. She didn't blame him, but she wasn't ready to go there. She'd tried more than once, but it made her itchy, and then she wanted to throw up. They needed to talk, but with Ella and everything else going on, finding time to talk was difficult.

"No."

"What do you think needs to happen to make sex between the two of you work?"

She shrugged. "I can't do it yet. I want to, but every time I try something goes haywire inside, and I freak out."

"Are you really freaking out, or are you having a response based on your past?"

She swallowed over the discomfort. "I'm having a response."

"We need to figure out what you need to make it easier on you."

She nodded, knowing it wouldn't be easy. Fear of Adam leaving her once he figured out how deficient she was made her scared. She didn't want to be dumped, but once Adam realized she'd been used up by those guys, he would be pissed. She should have told him how bad it had been. A part of her hoped he would have guessed, and she wouldn't have to speak about it, but it looked like she would have to tell him more about what had gone on when she'd been held captive.

"I know Adam had planned to come in with you, but then life got difficult with their travel and then the baby. It's time for him to join you in a session."

She nodded, knowing her therapist was right. The idea of opening up to the man scared her. She didn't want him to know everything, but him not knowing was part of the problem. She'd changed. If she wanted to stay with Adam, she needed to tell him all the things she'd suffered.

Adam came home later than usual. He seemed off, like there was something he wanted to talk about but didn't know how to broach the subject. She danced around their need to talk, not saying anything before bed.

When he stretched out beside her, the weight of the unsaid words pressed down. She turned to face him, and he rolled toward her. Desire sparked, but she feared her reaction. She should be over this by now. It had been months, and she'd been in therapy for months, too. There was just something in her brain preventing her from moving forward.

Her fingers drifted over his face before she then leaned in, kissing him, forcing herself to do this. Just once, that's all it might take to get over this. Then the next time wouldn't be so bad. She moved closer, praying it was quick, and then she wouldn't have to worry about it any longer.

His hands were on her. Touching wasn't too bad. She could do this and she wouldn't freak. Her therapist would hate the word *'freak out'* echoing in her mind.

Her respiration rate increased as her mind spun. The hands on her body turned demanding, or had they? Her thoughts were untrustworthy. Adam was still touching her gently, but the memories of those guys forcing her kept playing through her mind.

Adam reached between them, and his hand was in her underwear, grabbing her ass. She squirmed, trying not to remember what had been done to her. Panic built. Adam's hand moved under her shirt to her breast. She wanted to hold it together. The memories were too close. She screamed and then jumped up, racing to the bathroom.

Archer blew out a breath filled with all the frustration he'd been holding in. He wanted Candace, no question, but she had issues. He knew what they stemmed from. The image of her lying on the ground, her body bloody and bruised, came to mind. They'd raped her in the worst possible way. She wouldn't get over the abuse quickly. He had to be more patient.

In his mind, he knew he needed to give her time, but his cock wanted her. He woke so many times hard and horny for her. He had wild dreams of nearly pornographic sex with Candace. Not that he wanted to get super dirty with her, he would settle for simple vanilla missionary style. She was dealing with PTSD, and he needed to be patient.

She retched in the bathroom and he hesitated to give her a moment. His heart ached for her. She had to deal with too much, and it had almost destroyed her, but she'd survived. Now he had to help her get through this.

He opened the door to the bathroom. She sat on the floor, legs bent, head resting on her arms wrapped around her knees. The soft sound of crying wafted over him. Her body shuddered as he dropped to the floor beside her.

Thick pain wafted off her. She didn't deserve this. No one deserved this, except for maybe those assholes who had tried to hurt her, they deserved this.

He loved her, no question, he just had to help her get through the pain. It may take months or years, but he wouldn't give up.

"I'm sorry." Her voice was weak and sounded pathetic.

Pain filled his chest. He wanted to take all of her hurt away and give her relief, but she needed time, too. He measured his words before he spoke. "Don't worry. It's okay."

"No, it's not."

"Candace, it is. I don't have to have that."

She turned her head and shot him an infuriated look. "I want to."

"I know." She had wanted him, but the reality of her situation made it difficult. "How about we set up that appointment with your therapist? This time I'm sure nothing will get in the way. We'll go in and talk together."

Candace nodded slowly, doubt filling her mind. If she didn't have sex with him soon, he would find someone else. His hard-on pressed against her. Desire swirled between them, but the knowledge scared her. If only she hadn't been abducted by the group and abused, but then she wouldn't have ever met Archer.

Sadness grew and hung on to her, not letting her go though they went back to bed and sleep. She set up an appointment with Archer for a week later. Her time spent with Ella seemed to make life better. She enjoyed playing with the baby, experiencing all her milestones. Sugar was doing great and was happy to see Ella at the end of each day. Ella smiled every time her daddy came in, even on those days she was having trouble adjusting emotionally; she still had a smile for daddy.

Candace talked about Molly, or tried to though she didn't really know the woman. She figured telling Ella about Molly was the right thing to do. It was tough, though. The baby had never met her mother and wouldn't be able to comprehend what Candace was talking about.

On Wednesday evening, she took Ella up to a restaurant where the guys were eating dinner. The music wasn't loud when she walked in. Ella loved seeing the group of men Dion worked with. The guys would pass her around and feed her. They all talked and cooed to her like they were doting grand-parents or something.

When Candace stepped into the back room of

the place, a woman was straddling Archer's lap. He was facing the other way, so he didn't see Candace. Her heart stopped for a second. The guys were all laughing and seemed to be having a good time. Then one of the guys glanced up and sobered.

She had to drop off Ella, then she was out of there. She would sleep in her car, but she wouldn't ever spend the night at Archer's place again. How long had he been doing this? How many women was he fucking? She couldn't even blame him since she wasn't willing to have sex, and he needed it. There'd been little doubt in her mind this would happen. She had just wished he would have waited until he ended it with her first.

# CHAPTER 14

Archer wasn't in the mood for Lyla's antics. She'd been after him for the last year, but he'd put her off. He knew better than to sleep with this woman because her interest hadn't been at normal levels. Instead, she seemed almost frantic to have him. He had little doubt if he had sex with her, she would find a way to trap him.

She wouldn't leave him alone. When she'd come in and seen him, she'd tried to get him to go to the back. When that didn't work, she'd sauntered over to their table and sat on his lap, trying to get a rise out of him. He had no desire to be taken advantage of by her. Sure, he liked her body, but there was so much more to living and being with someone than just the way their body looked. He had to like the person, and he didn't like Lyla.

"Get off," he'd said more than once. She'd ignored him. Hitting women wasn't right, and he never would, but this woman wouldn't leave him alone. He tried to get her off his lap, but he feared hurting the woman. He needed to do something, but he wasn't sure what.

Of course, the guys were giving him hell. They knew he wasn't interested in Lyla and never would be. She was too desperate, too needy, and she made it known she wanted to marry a SEAL. Archer was about to stand up when Flip's face changed. He met Archer's gaze, panic flashing.

"Get off me," Archer growled. Instead of moving, Lyla ground against him, shoving her breasts in his face. Disgust filled him.

"You don't want that," Lyla purred. "Come on, I'll let you take me from behind."

Archer shoved his chair back and stood, trying to get disentangled from Lyla and not hurt her. Out of the corner of his eyes, he saw Candace. He turned and met her angry gaze. Lyla still clung to him like a wet rag, and no matter how much he tried to get away, she was stuck to him like glue.

"Candace," Archer said as she placed Ella's carrier

next to Sugar. She dropped the diaper bag and was headed out by the time he got rid of Lyla.

"I fucked him last night," Lyla called out then laughed when Candace's shoulders stiffened.

Candace ran. Her position was better than his. He had to move around a table, then dodge a group of women who'd just stepped into the bar. By the time he made it out to the street, Candace was gone. Shit, how had she gotten here and where had she gone? She couldn't be far.

"Fuck," Archer growled.

"Hey, we'll get her back."

Flip was beside him and tried to comfort Archer with a slap to his back, but Archer wanted none of it. He brushed off Flip's hand and let out a roar.

"Goddammit. She won't be back. All I wanted was a good woman, and now she's gone all because of that…that—" The door opened, and Lyla stepped out and headed his way.

"Forget her. I'm the one for you." Lyla was trying to look coy or flirty, but he didn't care.

"Go to hell," he growled. "I don't like you one bit. I'm in love with her."

Lyla tried for a pout. "You don't mean that."

"Fuck you," Archer said as he headed back inside. He wanted to run away, but he owed it to his team to stick around. They were eating dinner together and had only ordered drinks. This was their night to hang out, but it was the last place he wanted to be.

Lyla's hand landed on his arm. He brushed off her touch. He had just opened the door when Lyla jumped on his back.

"What are you doing?" Archer screamed as he tried to get rid of her.

He growled as she clung to him, fighting to keep hold. Flip pried her off his back as the restaurant manager came out.

"What is going on?" the guy asked.

"She won't leave me alone. I've told her I'm not interested, but she won't get off me," Archer said.

The manager turned to Lyla and narrowed his gaze. "Is what he said true?"

"He's a liar," Lyla pouted. "We've been together for years."

"She's lying," Flip said. "He's tried to get rid of Lyla for almost a year, but she keeps coming back like a bad case of the clap."

Lyla turned on Flip and tried to punch him, but he ducked out of the way. It was kind of funny to watch, but Archer didn't feel like laughing. Candace had walked out on him, and he needed her in his life. She needed him, too. They were good together, or could be. He wanted to have her near and never let her go.

The manager gasped then pointed to the lot. "You," the guy swung his finger to Lyla. "Get out and don't come back. These men are paying customers, and you're not welcome here. Seriously, don't you know that no means no?"

Lyla's mouth hung open, but Archer didn't care. They headed inside, where he hoped he would find some advice to help him get Candace back.

"You okay?" Sugar asked when Archer sat down.

"I don't know. I can't lose her."

"What's been going on?" Slayer asked.

Archer closed his eyes and shook his head before opening them to look at his friends. He should have told them more before now. "She's having some bad PTSD. Whatever happened to her over there is fucking with her mind." Archer wiped his hand over his face. "I don't know what to do."

"Go after her," Slayer said.

"I don't know how it would do any good. What if it pushes her away?"

Slayer stood and crossed his arms over his chest. "Go."

Archer nodded. Thick fear filled him, leaving him

almost not able to breathe. "I'll catch you all tomorrow."

"I'm going with you," Slayer said.

Archer opened his mouth to protest, but Slayer was beside him, pulling him along. "We're not letting her leave you."

They drove over in Archer's truck. Worry about missing her stayed with him. Why hadn't he raced after her? What if she really took off and he lost her?

Traffic slowed them, but when he arrived at his house, she was visible inside. He rushed in, and Slayer followed close behind.

"Candace," he called out as he opened the door. "Please don't leave."

She had her bag out, and her clothes halfway packed. Anger twisted up her features, and tears filled her eyes.

"I thought you were different. I thought you were special." Tears raced down her cheeks. He was supposed to be different for her, but he wasn't. He was the same type of jerk she could find anywhere. Defeat sucked at his soul. He may take down bad guys, but he was a loser where women were concerned.

"I'm sorry you saw her doing what she was."

"You're sorry I saw her? So you were just going to

hide an affair? Hell, it's not even an affair because we aren't having sex. So I guess you can do whatever you want." Candace threw up her arms and then growled before she turned back to packing her bag.

Archer blew out a breath, trying to remain calm. "I'm not having sex with anyone."

"Yeah, right," Candace spit out. "You're a guy. You have sex."

"I take commitments seriously." Archer wanted her to understand.

"We don't have any commitments."

"I may not have voiced it, but I am committed to you. I want us to work." Archer was ready to get down on his knees and beg. He'd never begged before, but today he would. He would beg and plead for Candace to stay.

"You're not giving him a fair chance," Slayer said.

Candace spun and faced Slayer. She put her hand on her hip and stared up at him. "Why are you even here? I don't need some overgrown asshole telling me what to do."

Archer had never seen anyone stand up to Slayer the way his woman was. The pride he felt mixed with the sadness of the situation. She wasn't his woman. He may want and need her, but she wasn't his.

"I'm here to make sure you hear him out."

She frowned at Slayer then huffed out a breath. "What does that even mean?"

"This." Slayer stepped closer, and for a moment Archer feared what he would do. "You haven't even heard what she was doing in Archer's lap."

"It's obvious, isn't it? She was grinding on him."

"Was he touching her?" Slayer asked.

Candace's lips sealed shut as her gaze swung to him, indecision all over her face. He had hope. It wasn't much, but there in her eyes he saw the flicker of something he could hold on to.

"Why were all of you laughing?" Candace spit back.

"It was obvious Archer didn't want her attention, but she kept at it. What else do you expect us to do? If we hit a woman, we're going to jail. We can't get into bar fights or blow off steam like other guys. We're held to a higher standard. Archer's only option was to wait her out. Any other guy would have shoved her off his lap, and she would have pouted then found someone else to pester. If Archer had pushed her off his lap, I can guarantee he would be in jail."

Candace's lips thinned as she looked from Slayer to him. Maybe Slayer's words were breaking through her ice. He knew they had a lot to work through. She needed to trust him, but he needed to trust her, too.

"Please, can we talk about this?"

She frowned, and her eyes narrowed as her brows bunched. "I can't stay here tonight."

"Sleep at Sugar's place. He won't bug you, and it will be a safe place to stay." Archer hoped she took him up on the offer.

She looked at her bag then the floor. Her brows pinched so tight a deep line developed between her eyebrows. "I don't know."

"Please," Archer begged.

The anger coming off her was intense. She had endured too much already. For a moment, he feared he'd lost out totally, then she finally nodded.

"I'll talk to you, but not now."

"We still have therapy tomorrow afternoon. We can talk then."

Her lips turned down and she shook her head. "I don't know if I want you there."

"Please. We need to talk." He held his breath, waiting for her to agree to talk at therapy. She would have to give him a chance. She had seen him in a bad situation, but that wasn't who he was. He didn't want to be with some random woman from a bar, he wanted to be with Candace for life. With her by his side, he knew he would have a purpose every day to come home to. All the bad in the world wouldn't matter if he had Candace at home.

Candace gave him one small nod, and his heart soared. She still didn't want to stay with him, so Archer drove her over to Sugar's house. She let herself in, not even waving as she slipped inside. He wanted to run up the steps and tell her to come home. He had to win back her trust before they could become more. She was the most important person in his life, now he just had to show her.

# CHAPTER 15

Candace didn't want to talk to Adam. Her mind had twisted over the image of that woman sitting on Adam's lap. He could have dislodged her. He should have done something.

That bitch had been grinding up against him like they were dating. Heck, even if she and Adam were dating, she would never act so brazen in public. How close were Adam and the woman?

Sugar had been careful to not say anything about Adam. He was being nice, and she had little doubt she would have to find a new place to live soon. She didn't want to back out on her promise to Sugar, though. Ella had to come before her broken heart.

She arrived at the therapist's office, ready to tell Adam it was over. The pressure to have sex in addition to everything else was too much. She had received the email about Cal's death days ago, but she'd been busy and hadn't opened it. Now she knew all three of the guys she'd been held captive with in Iran were dead. She took the news hard. Mike and Greg weren't nice, but Cal had been kind of decent. He hadn't tried to stop the assholes from raping her, but he wasn't as bad as Mike and Greg.

The door to the waiting room opened, and Adam stepped in. Her insides twisted. It was too much seeing him. She should have told him to not come. He was wearing a plain black T-shirt emphasizing the size of his biceps and well-fitting jeans. No question he affected her.

"Hey," Adam said as he took a seat across from her.

The door opened, and her therapist stepped out, not giving her time to say anything. "Good, you're both here. Let's go back."

Adam followed Candace into the office. She took a seat, trying to ignore Adam, but he was impossible to ignore. He exuded appeal even if he wasn't trying.

"I'm Dr. Foster. I've been working with Candace for a while. I'm glad you both are here. So, I'm noticing some tension. What is going on?"

Her face heated as her mind shifted to the image

of finding the woman grinding away on Adam's lap. She wouldn't ever be someone like that. Her sexual freedom had been taken from her when she'd been assaulted. She could only imagine what terrible things they'd done to her when she'd been passed out from the pain.

Tears came though Candace tried to squelch them. Adam moved to sit beside her, wrapping his arms around her. She wanted to hate him but she needed him.

Dr. Foster gave her a box of tissues, and she wiped her eyes and blew her nose, trying to calm. Her life was a mess and she just wanted everything to be good.

"Can you tell me what has you upset?" Dr. Foster asked.

"I can't have sex. And I know it will break us up," Candace said.

"You don't know what I want," Adam said. "You took the decision from me."

"How did she take the decision from you?" Dr. Foster asked.

"She left without giving me a chance to explain."

Adam's words were tinged with anger. She was angry, too, but not just at their situation, but the situation of her friends—well, fellow Marines. They were dead. She didn't know how Cal died, but she needed to find out.

"You were with some other woman!" Candace yelled as frustration ate at her.

"Hold on," Dr. Foster said. "Let's take a moment to breathe deeply."

Dr. Foster turned on some audio with soft music that instructed her to breathe in and out in measured beats. After the audio finished, Candace was a little calmer.

"Candace, can you state what happened without yelling?"

"I'm sorry. I showed up at the restaurant last night, and some woman was grinding away on Adam's lap."

"Adam, can you state what was going on?" Dr. Foster asked.

"The woman has been chasing me for over a year. I didn't want her touching me, but she slid onto my lap, and I was looking for a way to extricate myself without hurting her. I know I'm stronger than most, which means I have to be smart about how I get people to get out of my space."

"So this woman, have you ever been in a relationship with her?" Dr. Foster's question had Candace wondering.

"No," Adam said. "She has been hitting on me for over a year, and I'm not interested."

"Why?"

Archer didn't understand the question. "Why has she been hitting on me, or why am I not interested?"

"Both," Candace said.

Dr. Foster's lips quirked up. "Go ahead and answer."

He shook his head. He hadn't ever liked Lyla, but more importantly, he wanted a woman like Candace. How did he put his desires into words? "I'm not attracted to her. I don't know why she's hitting on me other than I'm a SEAL, and she wants one. I don't want her now because I have Candace, or I did."

He met Candace's gaze and tried for a smile. The hesitation in her eyes burned his soul. He should have done more to reassure his woman he cared about her.

Candace heard what Adam was saying, but fear hit hard. "What if I can't ever have sex?"

Adam dropped to his knees and faced her. His eyes were full of emotions. "Then we'll figure something out."

"You'd give up sex for me?" Shock coursed through Candace.

"I don't think you'll never be able to have sex. But

if it was the case, I would deal with it. I'm not a saint, and I've had plenty of sex, but when it lacks love, honestly, my hand is just as good. I don't want to waste my time having sex with someone who won't love me. I've been used—"

Candace scoffed and Adam's lips thinned.

"What? Do you think I can't have been used because I'm a SEAL? Women have told me they don't care about me, they just wanted to brag about having sex with one of us. You care about me."

Candace's heart squeezed. She did care about him. She cared possibly too much.

"Candace, do you care about Adam?" Dr. Foster asked.

She nodded. "I do. But I'm afraid."

"You can work through almost anything. We can do more EMDR therapy."

Candace blew out a harsh breath. "I just feel like such a failure, like I don't deserve to have someone who loves me."

"But you do," Adam said. "You're a good person, and I want you in my life."

"What if I can't ever have sex?" Candace feared what he would say. She watched his face, her stomach dropping as he frowned.

"There is more to love than sex. You make me

happy. I enjoy spending time with you. Yes, I want to have sex, but I would rather have you in my life without sex than sex without you."

She blinked at him, wondering if there was a way for them to move forward. Sex made or broke relationships. She wasn't ignorant.

"What are you thinking, Candace?" Dr. Foster asked.

"He won't stay with me once he realizes I can't get past my issues. I was thrown back into it when I got news Cal died."

Archer perked up. "Who is Cal?"

"One of the guys you rescued with me. They've all died in the last few months."

"What?" Panic filled Archer.

"Hold on. Before we get too far away on another subject..." Dr. Foster looked from her to Archer. "Maybe there's another way for you two to enjoy a physical relationship."

"What do you mean?" Candace asked.

"What if Archer masturbated in bed with you without the pressure of actual intercourse? What if you knew he wouldn't ask you to have sex? What if you were able to enjoy time in bed together, and there was intimacy, but no penetration?"

Candace's cheeks turned pink. Archer reached

out and took her hand. She didn't pull back, which gave him hope. If she would give them a chance, and maybe after a few more chances, some sweet loving, and with time perhaps they would work out.

Touching Adam gave Candace a thrill. She just feared penetration, or more precisely, being dominated. Her need for Adam grew, but she feared he would treat her like those men had. It was too hard to submit to sex and let him rule over her.

"I would be willing," Adam said.

"So, you weren't with her?" Candace had to make sure he wasn't faking it. Wasn't lying to her just to get her in bed.

He shook his head. "No. I want only you in my life. Women throw themselves at SEALs. Married or single, they don't care. But I vow to you I won't fall for that. I won't be with anyone else. If we can't make this work, I'll tell you. I will never cheat."

Could she trust him? Could she ever trust another person with her life? She'd been devastated by what had happened. It hadn't been Adam's fault, though. She might be strong enough to be with him, and he wouldn't use her.

"I'm afraid," Candace whispered.

"Of what?" Adam asked.

"That you'll see I'm not worth it."

"But you are."

"They used me. How can you want me if I don't even want to be me?"

Adam pulled her into his lap, holding her close. His lips were on her hairline and then her cheek, her jaw, then her lips. When he broke away, he stared into her eyes, fierceness shining through.

"Don't you get it?"

She shook her head. "No."

"They may have tried to destroy you, but you are valuable to me. I love you. You make my world better. I deal with so much bad in my work, so much horror. Week after week, I encounter the evil other people do to each other, but when I come home to you, it's like I can breathe again. I've found something amazing with you. Something wonderful. You make my life better. I love you, Candace. Not anyone else. I don't care what your limitations are. If I have a week, a month, or five decades with you, it won't be enough time. You make the world a better place for me, and I don't want to let you go."

This time the tears were mixed with happiness. No one had ever cared for her this way. With Adam believing in her, they would make it.

"It sounds like the two of you have a good foundation to build on. You both need to be patient with each other," Dr. Foster said.

"I can be patient," Adam said.

Candace nodded. "So can I."

Adam didn't let go of her even though she slid off his lap. They left the office together and headed home. The appointment had been something of a success. Maybe they could make it. She wanted Adam. But was wanting the man enough to keep him in her life or would she happen upon another woman pawing at her man just because he was a hot SEAL?

# CHAPTER 16

Candace said she wasn't ready to get on the bed and have Archer masturbate beside her. Instead he headed outside to water the plants. When he came inside, good smells were coming from the kitchen. He washed his hands and shot her a smile, wondering how to help her relax.

"Could you grab the milk?" Candace asked.

He reached into the refrigerator and grabbed it out. Candace was the most beautiful woman he'd ever seen. He liked working in the kitchen with her.

"Do you have any onion powder?" Her gaze met his, and he almost reached for her, but he had to give her space.

"Here you go," he said as he gave her the bottle of onion powder.

How would he fit Candace into his life? Being a SEAL had been everything to him. He loved his job, but he longed for more. So far, she fit perfectly. His team liked her, she didn't ask questions about his missions, and she made him feel wonderful. Was that enough for her?

"What are you thinking?" Candace's question made him glance up. He heated at the look in her eyes.

"That after we eat, we need to practice." It wasn't the only thing he'd been thinking, but it was at the top of his list.

She shoved the food into the oven. "It makes me nervous."

"You can be nervous. You want to know one thing few SEALs talk about?"

She washed her hands, then dried them on the towel before she turned to face him. "What?"

"We get nervous and scared, but we move past it and try to do our jobs anyway. We aren't inhuman, we've just grown to the point we push forward."

Anger flashed inside Candace and threatened to spill out. "Do you think I should just have sex even though it bugs me?"

He shook his head. "No, but we should try masturbating together tonight. Small steps."

The idea made her hot but also worried. What if she didn't get this right? Was there a right way to masturbate? The idea of rubbing one out with him staring at her was a little bizarre.

"Don't you think it's weird?"

He shrugged. "No. I want to be intimate with you. Even if you're lying in bed while I jack off, I'll take it."

A shudder ripped through her at the thought of Archer hard and waiting for her. She bit her lower lip then realized she hadn't set the timer. She opened the oven to check if the food was bubbling. It wasn't, so she set the timer for fifteen minutes.

"I need to shower," Adam called out as he headed to the bathroom.

Heat flashed. The idea of Adam naked in the shower was alluring. She could do this and not let the memories tumble over her. She needed to shower, too. Not that they would have sex, but she wanted to be clean if they did anything more than undress in front of each other. She glanced at the timer, seeing the food only had eleven minutes left. If she went into the shower right then, the food would be ruined.

Eating across from Adam, knowing what they were about to do, drove her crazy. She kept glancing at him, imagining him touching her, kissing her, loving her. She wanted the good thoughts and none of the bad.

After they finished eating, Adam said he would clean up the dishes, so she headed to the shower. Her hands were shaking, and she was having difficulty concentrating. When she came out of the bathroom, Adam was in the hallway. He took her hand and led her into the bedroom. This was weird. Would he kick her out if she didn't give him what he wanted? But Adam didn't seem to mind any of this. His lips were on hers, brushing gently over hers. Her hands shook as she ran them over his torso. Her fingers tingled as she grazed over his skin.

She tugged up the hem of his shirt. Adam grabbed the back of his collar, pulling the shirt over his head. His muscles were defined and beautiful with a dusting of hair over his chest that ran down the center of his body to his waist band.

She placed her palm over his heart, and her eyes flicked up to his. All she saw was caring and love. It spurred her on. She tugged off her shirt, which she'd just put on in the bathroom. Maybe she should have stayed naked and in a towel, but having clothes made her feel more powerful.

The spiral of bad thoughts started, but she pushed it away and concentrated on getting rid of Adam's pants. She undid the button and grabbed the key to the zipper. He sucked in air fast, drawing her gaze to his face. Heat filled his eyes, and his hands on her hips shook. She slowly lowered the zipper, watching his every move, seeing the passion fill his eyes.

She'd missed this. Missed the anticipation of making love to someone. When she'd been held prisoner in Iran, they'd not only taken her freedom, they'd taken pieces of her. She almost broke down, but they'd come so far.

The idea had been to masturbate in bed, but she wanted to continue exploring Adam. She needed to have the power touching him gave her.

With his zipper open, she shoved his pants low. He had on tight blue underwear, revealing his raging hard-on. A shiver worked through him, and she glanced up, seeing he was just as into her as she was into him.

He reached for her, but she pushed his hands away. "No, you go lie on the bed."

Archer's cock twitched. God, he wanted to be inside her, but he would take this at her pace. If that meant they only masturbated, then all they would do was masturbate. He tugged down the covers and stretched out, waiting for her.

He'd never met anyone as beautiful as she was. She had her shirt off but her pants on. Her breasts weren't too huge, but they were nicely sized in the black bra she had on. She sauntered around the bed, her eyes staying on him. When he moved, she paused. He had to keep still.

Candace glanced at the closet then moved quickly, grabbing out his robe. He didn't want his robe, but then she pulled out the long belt and moved to the bed. Her gaze went from the belt to him, then back to the belt.

"While I was…I can't stop the fear. I'm afraid I'll be dominated, and I won't be able to say no. Can I…"

He waited for her to continue, but she said nothing more. Archer lifted his hands over his head and crossed them at his wrists. "Tie me up. I'll do anything. I have handcuffs at work or zip ties. Anything you need to feel safe."

Candace heated as she looped the belt around his wrists and tied it tight, hoping it was enough to hold him. She tied the other end of the robe's belt to the headboard, pulling out all the slack. Adam couldn't move his arms, which meant he couldn't force her to do anything.

Her gaze slid down his body, taking in the tight muscles and silky skin. He had just enough hair to make him hotter, but not too much. Her tongue slid out, wetting her lips as she anticipated licking him.

Before everything had happened, she loved sex. She hadn't had a lot of partners, but she'd dated a few guys for longer than one or two months, and they'd eventually had sex. It had been wonderful. She wanted sex with Adam.

"I want to touch you," she whispered.

"Touch me wherever." Adam's voice was breathy. His eyes were half hooded as he stared at her. She still had her bra on and her pants. They needed to go, so she flicked off her bra and pushed her pants and underwear low before crawling onto the bed.

Adam's gaze stayed on her as she tugged at his underwear. His cock bobbed free. It was impossibly hard with a thick vein running down the underside. He was cut and beautiful. She leaned over and kissed the tip. He moaned, and his eyes rolled up in his head. She kissed and licked him, liking having him at her mercy.

Archer might die if she kept this up. He wanted to touch her and taste her pink nipples, but she was in control. He'd never been the type to give up control in sex, but with Candace, he would do anything. His dick might explode if she kissed him again. He thought of sliding into her and almost came.

She was touching and kissing him, driving him crazy. It would be easy for him to break free, but he didn't want to disappoint Candace. He would stay still, allowing her to torture him with her body if it made her happy.

"I need something, but you can't move."

He met her gaze and nodded. She was giving him such exquisite agony, pushing him to the edge of sanity. "Anything for you."

Candace straddled him and he glanced down, staring at her pussy with neatly trimmed hair. She hadn't shaved, but it was obvious she kept the hair under control. She grabbed his cock and brushed it over her opening up to her clit. His orgasm teased at his control, driving him crazy. He gasped as his heart raced. Then Candace sat up straighter before she lowered.

He cried out as he forced himself not to pump up. His whole body shuddered as she lifted, then lowered again. His hands ached to hold her, but she was in control, and he wouldn't disappoint her.

"Oh, God, Candace."

She lifted one more time, then lowered. She was

hot and wet and he fit perfectly as she sank down. Her breasts were squished together by her arm and it was the picture of sex.

His breath caught and he came. The orgasm ripped through him. He may have blacked out. When he could think again, he blinked up at her, trying to focus as she reached between them, brushing her fingers over her clit. She moaned and bucked as she came. Her orgasm brought him back to life. The excitement of being tied up while she rode him was a huge bonus.

She met his gaze and quirked up one eyebrow. "You're getting hard again."

"Oh God, this is too much."

"I can't untie you." Candace worried her lip with her teeth. She wanted more but fear still drove her.

"I'm okay if you don't undo the belt. I mean, it's tough, but I can handle it."

She paused, and he started shaking his head. "What do you mean?"

"Please don't stop. I'll do whatever you want. You're in charge."

Tears gathered in her eyes as she lifted her hips. She lowered and his whole body shuddered as he gasped.

The power she had over him made her insides

tighten and tingle. She watched his face as she moved slowly. He was gasping for breath, his body shaking. She slowed even more, watching as he struggled.

This was torture for him. It was obvious by the way his face twisted as she rode him.

Candace sped up, and then Adam bucked his hips. She didn't try to stop him. Instead, she held on, allowing him to go as fast as he needed. The friction built between them. She leaned over, and his cock hit her in the exact right spot. She was so close to coming.

Adam pumped up twice more. It was enough for her to explode with bliss. When she opened her eyes, a single tear had leaked out of the corner of Adam's eye.

Her heart went out to him. She reached for the belt tying his hands and let him go. Adam moved fast, flipping her. A gasp escaped her lips, but he didn't trap her or hurt her.

"Candace, I swear by all I am I will love you forever. Anything you're uncomfortable doing, I'll stop. All you have to do is say the word. I promise to protect you."

"Was it too much?"

He shook his head then lowered enough to kiss

her. "Heck no. My God, that was the best orgasm I've ever had. You took me to a place I didn't know I could go."

"So, you liked me dominating you?"

"God, yes. If it's what you need, I'm in for it."

She sat up, and he moved so she had space around her. "I'm not saying I won't want something different later."

"Whatever you need."

She bit her lower lip as her face heated. "That was good."

"Holy hell, you were freaking amazing."

"I didn't expect us to have sex. I wasn't even sure I could get through you masturbating." She moved closer to him and kissed his lips. "I want to have sex again. Maybe not this week, and I'll need to mentally prepare for it, but I want this between us."

He drew in a shaky breath and nodded. "I would be happy to be tied to the bed again."

She stood and headed into the bathroom. He was right behind her, helping her into the tub. They showered together though they'd just cleaned up. That evening he was practically waiting on her. They fell asleep in the same bed, him holding her tightly.

The next morning she snuggled under the covers,

not wanting to leave Adam. They'd had such a good day before, and she didn't want it to end.

"Time for wakey wakey," Archer said as he stood and headed to the bathroom.

"Ugh, I wish we could stay in bed all day."

"Same. But you've got a group session at the VA this morning, and I've got work. Who is looking after Ella?"

"Caroline and Alabama have her until ten. Then I'm taking her to the botanical gardens. I know she's young but being out will help her develop."

"Just be safe."

"Got it," she said as she stepped into the bathroom, admiring the view of Adam's naked backside.

He turned and his lips quirked up in a smile as he handed her the mouthwash. She rinsed then spit before turning to watch him step into the shower.

"You're awfully sexy, mister."

"So are you. I liked what we did yesterday."

She chuckled then brushed her teeth, thinking about how much fun Ella would have looking at the flowers. Some people would say she was lame her taking a baby to a garden, but the wind on her face and the sounds would stimulate Ella.

"I will be. We'll be cautious."

"We need to get you a vehicle," Adam said.

Annoyance flicked through her. "I'm fine."

"I think I'll start looking today for something reliable."

She didn't want him to have to do everything for her. "Adam, I'm okay. I can look for my own car."

"I know, but I want to help. If I can find something affordable and clean, will you look at it?"

She shrugged. "As long as it has space for Ella. Once you guys deploy, I'll have her full-time."

Adam leaned against the counter. "Is it too much?"

Candace smiled. Ella had changed everything. "Surprisingly, no. I like having her around. It's weirdly calming. At first, I thought I wouldn't be able to handle it, but I enjoy being a caregiver. It's so different from what the Marines were. I have a purpose now, and I like it."

Adam moved to her and leaned in but didn't kiss her. He wanted her to close the distance. She moved and pressed her mouth to his. He took control by swiping his tongue over her lips. She opened, and his tongue delved inside, tasting her. She opened more for him and leaned her head back. An image of her riding him filled his mind, and his cock filled out. Archer had work, and she had to leave.

He ended the kiss and stepped back. “I hope you have a wonderful day today.”

She lifted up on her toes and kissed his cheek. “I’m sure I will. I’ll call you once I get to Dion’s house.”

She stepped into gear and grabbed a mug of coffee before she dressed, taking sips of the black liquid in between pulling on her clothes. She’d loved wearing her uniform but wearing comfortable jeans and a nice T-shirt while caring for Ella was so much better.

While getting dressed, she ordered a shared ride to pick her up. Adam was right, she needed to get a car. Her hand still bothered her, but driving wouldn’t be too bad.

After a kiss goodbye, she ran out to the car. The woman driving didn’t say much, which suited Candace fine. Lost in thought, she wondered if she should contact anyone in the Marines to find out what had happened with Cal.

They were in traffic, stopped at a light, when a black van pulled up beside them. She looked away, not liking the intense look the driver was giving her. She was about to say something when the van pulled out ahead of her driver and blocked them in. The door beside Candace was tugged open, and she was pulled out. She kicked at the man and screamed, but he had her up over his shoulder and was racing away from the car.

Candace fought to break free, but in seconds they had her flat on her back in the van, the air gone from her lungs and her head swimming. She cried out for help and tried to scramble away, but a burst of electricity hit, and she flopped to the metal floor, unable to move.

# CHAPTER 17

Archer dropped into the chair across from Flip and sipped his coffee, his mind on the previous day. There was something off, something not right tugging at his thoughts.

"What's your look for?"

He shook his head at Flip's question then sipped more coffee. "It's nothing."

"Ha!" Flip let out a bark of laughter. "I've seen that look before. Something is baking in your brain."

He met Flip's gaze, wondering how much he should say. "Candace said something, and I don't know…"

Flip grabbed a mug and poured some coffee. "Tell me."

Archer heated as an image of her above him

flashed through his mind. He pushed away the erotic thoughts and concentrated on the few seconds in the therapist's office were bugging the heck out of him.

"We were at her therapist's office when she said the three other guys who we'd rescued had been killed."

Flip's eyebrows shot up as he lowered to the chair he'd been in earlier. "In action?"

"I don't know. I don't think so."

"You didn't ask?" Flip's question sounded like an accusation.

He shook his head then stood as frustration ground through him. "No. We were deep into some stuff, and then I forgot."

"You forgot." Flip looked at him like he'd lost his mind. "Must have been some deep shit for you to forget. You usually don't let stuff slip."

Guilt twisted through him. Flip was right. He didn't usually let things slip. He needed to get a grip. "We need to figure out what happened to those guys." Archer tapped the table. "Come on, we've got some work."

They sat down at the computer and began searching for the names of the guys they'd rescued on the mission where they'd saved Candace. Sugar came in and asked what they were doing.

"Yesterday, Candace informed me the three guys we rescued with her were dead." Archer pulled up information on Mike Kallas' death. "Hit and run."

Before Archer had been worried, now he was downright scared. He pulled up information on Greg. Flip whistled, and Sugar shook his head.

"I don't believe in coincidences," Sugar said.

"Looks suspicious, doesn't it?" Archer asked.

"More than suspicious. A hit and run, one of the guys taken out into the woods and shot. Look at the third one," Flip said.

He found the information for Cal's death and stared at the screen, not believing what he was reading. He'd been murdered in his own house. It seemed impossible.

"Where's Candace?" Flip asked.

"Group session." He stood and pulled out his phone.

"You'd best call her now," Sugar said.

Archer pulled out his phone and dialed, getting her voicemail. She wouldn't answer if they were in the middle of a session, right?

"It's me, Archer. Call me."

He hung up. His worry blew into a full-grown panic. He wanted to hear from Candace. Would she call him back?

"Can you call anyone?" Dion asked.

He shouldn't call around about his woman. It showed a significant lack of trust. He was trying to rebuild her confidence. Would she believe he was worried, or would she think he was trying to take over her life? He couldn't do nothing.

"I don't know." Archer had never been so indecisive in his life. He palmed his phone before he started calling around, looking for Candace.

Three calls in and he was eventually connected to the place where she had her group sessions. "It's Adam Culver. I just want to make sure Candace got there okay."

"Sir, we can't interrupt a group session, and we can't give out personal information over the phone."

"Listen, she could be in danger. Do you see her name on the list of people who have checked in? I just want to make sure she got there. If her name isn't there, call the police. She should be there by now. I need to know." Archer knew he sounded agitated. This was impossible. He should have driven her this morning, but it was in the opposite direction from the base, and she said she was fine getting there herself. God, he was such a fool.

"Hey, Archer, look at this."

Sugar waved him over. Archer gripped his phone,

anger churning at the situation. Why couldn't he get any answers? Sugar pointed to the computer screen. The footage was grainy, but it was apparent the van had done something like take someone.

The video almost looked staged, and he was about to tell Sugar he was barking up the wrong tree when he realized the woman was wearing what Candace had been wearing.

"Sir, I don't see her name on the list."

"Shit, she's been abducted." Archer hung up, his head spun, and his mouth went dry. She'd been taken right from under his nose. How had he missed these crucial clues? The three guys she'd been held with in Iran were dead. Shit. He should have paid better attention.

"Fuck, I don't know what to do."

"I'll call Tex and find out if he knows what to do," Dion said.

Archer cursed to himself. Why had he allowed his pride to distract him? Why hadn't he known those guys had been murdered? Their deaths had happened in different cities and two different states. Law enforcement wouldn't have connected them.

"Hey, Archer, Tex is emailing us some information. We might have a lead."

"Shit, this freaking sucks," Archer said.

"We'll get her back," Flip voiced. "I need to inform the team what is going on."

Archer watched Sugar type away. He read Tex's email, praying the information led to something. If he didn't find Candace, he wasn't sure what he would do with his life.

# CHAPTER 18

Candace forced the tears away, vowing not to break as the men screamed at each other. Something hadn't gone right when they'd taken her. Their words didn't make sense. Farsi? The memory of being held in Iran, the torture she'd endured, came back in full force, haunting her. Those men had damn near destroyed her. She would fight until her last breath. If it took every ounce of energy she had, she would work to destroy them.

Before, she hadn't believed how evil those men would be. She knew these men were less than human. They had to be the ones who had killed Mike, Cal, and Greg. She wasn't close with any of the three, but they didn't deserve to die, and not by these jerks.

Candace had no doubt if she'd been in her own car, she still would have been ambushed. At least they hadn't come after her when Adam had been around or when she had Ella. If they'd been hurt, she never would have forgiven herself.

The men turned on her, and one of them came at her with a metal pipe. She cringed as he swung, hitting her in the leg. The bone didn't crunch, but if he used force, it would break.

Her hands were cinched behind her, leaving her open for attack. She prayed her death came fast and easy. If they would just shoot her, this would be over with.

She closed her eyes and brought up an image of Adam. At least she'd had him for a little while. She should have slept with him before. He was nothing like these men. The fear of him dominating her, never listening to her needs, had been way off. Adam was a caring man, and he would have been a caring lover.

The men grabbed her and pulled her up. She fought their hold, but she was no match for three men. They were dragging her into a room with a cot. The last thing she wanted was to be forced to have sex with them. She had lived through hell once, and she wouldn't do it again.

Candace lifted her leg and stomped down on the side of one of the guy's legs. He cried out in pain. She wouldn't be their toy. They wouldn't get any pleasure out of her. She would make sure they knew she meant business.

The guy stepped in front of her, and she kneed him in the groin. He dropped to the ground, writhing in pain. A smile crossed her lips. She was happy for a moment until the guy next to her punched her. It had been worth it, though. She struggled to break free of their hold. She wanted to tell them to go to hell, that she wouldn't be used this way. No way would she allow these men to take advantage of her.

The guy on the ground stood and came at her. Rage shone in his eyes as he moved in, wrapping his hands around her neck. He cut off her air supply, but she was okay with that. If she died, then she wouldn't feel their hands on her.

* * *

ARCHER WANTED TO SCREAM. THEY HAD NO CLUE where Candace was being held. No one had come forward claiming responsibility or stating they'd taken her. It worried him. If they started communicating, it would mean she wasn't dead or most likely wasn't dead. If they stayed silent, she was probably gone.

A shiver snaked through him, and he closed his eyes, not wanting to think of her death. She was his life. God, he'd screwed up.

"Fuck!" Archer yelled.

"Hey, we're closing in on where she is. Don't worry. We'll figure this out," Flip said.

"I'm falling apart," Archer growled.

"We know. That's why I'm lead right now. Go splash some water on your face. We'll handle this."

Archer knew he was more of a distraction to the team than a help. They needed him to be calm, not freaked out. After splashing water on his face he stared at his reflection in the mirror. Distraction had caused him to lose focus. Candace had known about the dead guys but he'd been too interested in sex. Now she would suffer because of his lack of attention to details.

"Hey, Archer," Flip called out.

He moved fast, running back into the main room. "What's up?"

"We're moving out. Tex found the location. The van was spotted heading west on highway 905."

"Shit, what are they doing out there? They could be hours away and into Mexico." Panic filled Archer.

"Tex says they stopped near an area with warehouses about forty-five minutes away."

Archer almost stayed back, but this was his woman, and these were his men. His team couldn't operate in an official capacity in the US, but the rules wouldn't stop them from moving in on the assholes and getting Candace back.

The drive seemed to take forever. He hated that she'd been with these jerks for any amount of time. She had to be scared. After everything, she had to be scared to death. He would never forgive himself for allowing anything to happen to her. If he found these men, he might just kill them. They didn't deserve to live. He'd do whatever it took to take them down, even if it killed him.

* * *

CANDACE BLINKED A FEW TIMES, TRYING TO GET HER bearings. The guy had choked her, and she guessed she'd passed out. They'd dragged her into a room filled with weapons. When they'd first shown up, she'd gotten a glimpse of the warehouse. It looked like a normal food or paper goods storage center.

The unit they'd brought her into was at the end, and she doubted anyone would hear her yelling.

The room they had her in now looked like the arsenal at a Marine base. They had way too many guns and way too much ammunition to be anything other than a terrorist set up. If these jerks weren't found out by the authorities, they could do massive damage.

No way would she allow that to happen. Perhaps she could grab one of the guns. It was just a thought, and probably wouldn't happen, but she let the fantasy play out in her mind for a moment.

Her hands were stuck. The assholes had attached zip ties to her wrist and then secured her to a pipe on the far wall. With no way to get free of the pipe, she slumped against the wall. Depression loomed.

They would come back for sex. When they did, she would have to fight to get free. What if she pretended to like it, then surprise them and kill whoever was raping her? How would she kill them? She had no clue how any of this would work, but she had to try.

If only Adam knew where she was. His team would disable these men and not get killed in the process. If she had real access to a gun, she wouldn't be killed.

Never again. She would never be someone's fuck toy ever again. She started counting the guns and was at seventy-two when the door opened. Only one guy stepped in. He was talking to her in Farsi, which meant she didn't understand a word of what he was saying.

"I don't understand you," she said dryly.

The guy's hand flew, and the sound of his palm across her cheek reverberated around the room. It took her a few seconds to recover. She sneered at the guy, anger filling her. It would be good to hit him.

In her mind, she fought back even though she was forced to take whatever he dished out. The guy hit and kicked at her. She protected her head as much as possible.

The door opened, and one of the dude's friends came in. They stepped close, whispering as they glanced at her a few times in their discussion. Lust turned their eyes dark. It wasn't at all like the love she'd seen from Adam. If she ever made it back to him, she wouldn't waste time worried about how he would treat her. She knew he would always treat her like a queen. She would welcome sex with Adam because he would always put her first.

The men cut the zip ties holding her. She didn't move for a moment. Based on their stance, they were ready for her to attack. Her lack of trying seemed to surprise them. Then they laughed like jerks making a visit to their first-ever titty bar. But she didn't plan to take their abuse without a fight.

One of the guys came close, and she lifted her leg, her knee striking true. He didn't back away fast enough and dropped to the ground. They would overpower her soon enough, but for now, she was on a mission to destroy these guys.

She moved fast, grabbing a gun. It wasn't loaded, but she had a weapon. The man left standing shot her a grin then circled to her left. He lunged, and she moved away. She realized a little too late he'd cut her access off to the door.

Panic rose. This was her end. She wouldn't make it out of this room packed with guns and a tiny cot where some terrorist act was planned and would be carried out. No one would find her because if they knew about this place, they already would have closed them down.

She hoped Adam knew she loved him. He needed to have a long and happy life. He did so much for the country and the world, he needed happiness, and she wouldn't be there to give it to him.

# CHAPTER 19

A tiny car driven by an older woman who had lost her license because of blindness set out to cross into Mexico one last time. She misjudged the distance between her and an eighteen-wheeler carrying a load of syrup. She overcorrected, sliding off the highway and down a drainage ditch. The driver of the truck couldn't control his load. The syrup spilled on the roadway caused two more wrecks.

When Archer and his guys drove up on the mess, traffic was at a standstill. "What the hell?" Archer pounded on the dashboard and then turned in his seat. "How far are we?"

"We're one point five miles," Flip said.

"We could run there faster," Sugar said.

"Fuck." Archer took off his seatbelt and turned to

the guys in the back seats. Sugar and Black lifted their eyebrows as if to ask if he was ready. Flip was driving and couldn't abandon the truck. Mist was driving the other car with Slayer.

"Let's go," Sugar said. "We need to save her. We don't know what they are doing, but if she's alive, she won't last long. They killed those other guys without hesitation."

Black pulled out his phone as he undid his seatbelt. "I'm calling Slayer. We'll run over. Find a place to park and then come find us. Mist will do the same."

"Shit, I hate getting left behind." Flip tapped Archer on the shoulder before he opened the door to slip out. "Go get her."

Archer's throat closed as he nodded. He had to remain calm. The last thing Candace needed was him fucking this up.

"Let's go," Archer choked out.

They probably looked concerning to people around them, but Archer couldn't bother with what they looked like. The four of them took off, running across the other four lanes of traffic. They ran across the field, the four of them keeping pace like they were on a mission overseas. He knew they were drawing attention, but they were four military men.

He hoped people would ignore them. Military guys did crazy stuff all the time. He had to gamble on people thinking they were doing something crazy.

"Archer, you're too close to this, and Flip is back there. I'm in charge," Slayer said. "Turn your radios on."

Black laughed as he flipped his on. "I outrank you all. But I get it. Experience counts."

They moved from the open field, across another street and into the complex of warehouses where they believed Candace was being held. He hoped Candace was being held here. If they'd somehow taken off with her, transporting her across the border or headed north into the USA, they would have a difficult time finding her.

His phone rang in his earpiece. He answered, praying this was good news. "Archer here."

"It's Flip. We pulled off the road and are on our way."

"Good. We'll be in position. Slayer is lead now."

"Good. Stay safe and bring her home."

The call ended as they neared the area where Candace was being kept. Slayer stopped them behind a warehouse one row over. "We need to check for cameras."

Sugar pulled out a mirror and moved it to look

around the corner. "Two cameras. They seem to have full coverage."

"Shit," Slayer said. "We'll have to assume they don't have anyone watching."

Slayer met Archer's gaze. His eyes narrowed. "I'm good," Archer said.

"I need you to be here, I'm circling to the right, and Sugar and Black are heading around to the left. We'll coordinate our entry. Archer, you hang back until we've entered then come in, guarding our six."

As much as he wanted to be there to rescue Candace, he knew he had to hang back."

"I have my lock pick," Black said.

"Good. You open us up. We can't breach like we normally would."

Archer squeezed Slayer's shoulder. "I know you'll get her."

Slayer gave a sharp nod before turning to head into the building. Hanging back and waiting was the hardest part. He didn't want to sit around doing nothing, but he had to for Candace. She deserved more than she'd ever gotten. This was total bullshit, and he freaking hated it.

"We're about a block away," Flip said over his earpiece.

Slayer's voice came over the waves. "We're breaching in three, two…"

Archer moved around the building, sliding into position as Flip and Mist came up beside him. They motioned their intentions, heading into the building before him. He was their backup. He would keep the heat off them if the cops showed up or if some curious security guard with a gun decided to get in the way.

"We're in and behind you," Mist said.

"I hear yelling," Slayer stated.

Archer wanted to know what was going on. He was dying to find Candace. He prayed she wasn't already dead. If she was, he would rip these guys apart.

Slayer moved into position, standing ready once Sugar slid open the door. They were operating in the USA. If they killed this guy, they would be tried for murder. There was no way around it. The repercussions would be far reaching. But losing his job was worth it if he saved Candace.

There was no way the cops would listen fast enough or be prepared to deal with whatever was going on in the next room. On his way through the warehouse, he'd seen the signs. This was a terrorist's den. They'd somehow made it into the USA and were operating here, just under the nose of the US Border Patrol. This cell wasn't hiding in some backwoods cabin, they were within miles of law enforcement meant to stop this from ever happening.

"Move," Slayer whispered. The radio system they used allowed them to speak with almost no volume, but the receivers amplified it, meaning all the guys heard his command.

Sugar pushed the door wide, and Slayer rushed in, seeing the guy punching Candace. The terrorist stood and turned, but Slayer had moved to him in two long steps and pulled him off Archer's woman. He punched the man twice, stopping himself from beating the man to death.

Sugar and Black had the other guys cornered. They zip-tied their hands while Mist raced in and started working on Candace.

Archer made sure no sirens were coming their way, and he closed the door to the warehouse, locking it. He ran to the back where the guys were talking. When he stepped in, Mist was leaning over Candace. Archer moved to her, dropping to the ground beside her. She moaned and cracked open one swollen eyelid. Her lips twitched up, and she moaned again.

"Hey, love, we'll get you taken care of." Archer met Mist's gaze. "Have you called for an ambulance?"

"Not yet. I'm not sure how we'll explain this."

"Fuck." Archer looked around, seeing all the guns, the ammunition, the grenades, and the bombs. How the hell would they explain this? He had to get Candace to a hospital.

"I'm fine," Candace slurred.

His heart squeezed. She wasn't okay. She'd been beaten and blood oozed from a wound on her head. One arm seemed to be hanging at an odd angle.

"Can you walk?" Mist asked.

Anger filled Archer. Candace needed someone to take care of her, not make demands of her. He was about to say something when Candace tried to sit up. Mist moved to help her while Archer wanted to keep her lying down.

"Hold up, she's injured." Archer wanted to punch Mist for making her move.

"I'm okay," Candace said.

"Fuck, you're not. We need to get you medical attention." Archer was close to losing it.

"We need to call in the FBI," Slayer said.

"Call Creed," Archer barked.

Sugar made sure all three of the terrorists were

zip-tied and secured. They had Creed on speakerphone.

"Let me get this right. You six just happened to be out near Otay Mesa and just happened to see someone who looked like Candace being led into a warehouse. You stumbled in and found a cache of weapons and three terrorists who happened to be beating Candace. You caught the terrorist and saved Archer's woman?"

"That about sums it up, sir," Black said.

"Lieutenant Black, I hope you understand being an officer comes with a code of honor."

"Sir, it is my duty to serve the USA in truth and honor. I would never lie about a mission."

"Hmmm, you six are going to be the death of me."

"I'm sure the other SEAL team under your watch is as inventive as we are," Black said.

"Dammit, Black, you're not supposed to say shit like that," Creed barked. "Give me five minutes. I'll have a medical team there in a few. The FBI will arrive. When they get there, please play dumb. None of that inventive crap. Just be the stupid military guys they think you are, all brawn with no brains. I'll make sure whoever takes the lead in the FBI won't question you all."

"Thank you, sir," they all said.

"Just do your job. And guys," Creed said.

"Yes," Black answered.

"Thank you for saving the USA's ass once again. No doubt, you prevented a terrorist action on our soil. Of course, the official account won't have you mentioned, and you can't talk about this, but you six saved our asses."

Creed hung up, and they all breathed out a sigh of relief. Candace had her eyes closed while Archer held her hand. After a few seconds, the whop whop of a helicopter landing filled the area.

"I'll go look," Black said.

Archer appreciated how Black was taking charge, talking to Creed, taking the lead on seeing who was in the helicopter, doing what needed to be done. The man was leader material, he just needed the experience of being on the front lines in a SEAL unit. It would be hard to let him go, but Archer knew sometime in the next four years, Black would have a team and be leading it like a pro.

Candace coughed, and he glanced down, seeing her staring up at him. "Hey," she whispered.

"Your ride is here." He didn't want her to leave, but he needed to be here when the FBI arrived. This was his team, his men. He owed them the duty of sticking up for them if uncomfortable questions were asked.

"Will you come with me?"

His lips twisted into a wobbly smile. "I'll be there as soon as I can. I have to talk to the FBI. Once I'm done, I'll be by your side."

She nodded then lifted her hand, grabbing his shirt. He paused and leaned in closer.

"Kiss me."

His heart cracked in two at her request. "Of course, my love." He lowered and brushed his lips over hers. She was the best thing that had ever happened to him, and he hoped she never had reason to doubt him again.

Black led the medics in, and they strapped Candace to the stretcher. They were from the Navy base and didn't ask questions. Creed had pulled some big strings to get them out here to pick up Candace.

"We're taking her to the Naval Medical Center," one of the guys said as they headed out.

Archer stayed beside the stretcher until they had Candace loaded onto the helicopter. "I love you," he called out before stepping back. They lifted off seconds later. God, he wanted to be on that bird.

"She'll be okay," Black said.

"Thanks, man."

"For what?"

"Taking lead. You're a good man. I know we give you hell because you're new and an officer, but you'll be a great SEAL team lead in a few years. I hate to lose you, but I'll be glad to support your team."

Black slapped him on the back. "You're an awesome person to be training under. I will only be a good leader because you showed me how. Thank you."

Once back inside the warehouse, they made sure their story was straight. Archer said he would do the talking. The guys tried to tell him he didn't have to, but he was the lead, and he had to take responsibility for his team's actions.

Flip and Mist retrieved their cars while Sugar erased any video evidence of them being there. He also found all the other cameras and hacked into their storage systems, erasing the evidence of them being there. Then he shut the systems down for the next four hours.

About an hour later, there was a knock on the door. Archer opened it to find four FBI agents looking all serious and shit. He wished he was with Candace, but he had to answer their questions first.

"Good afternoon, gentlemen. I'm Agent Brock.

They informed me I shouldn't ask questions but I want to."

Archer gave him a tight smile but said nothing. They all stood there for half a minute, each group measuring the other.

"I'm guessing you were informed not to talk," Agent Brock said.

"Something like that," Archer spoke, knowing this agent wouldn't give them hell.

"I guess we'll have to take a look and figure out what we found."

"Be careful. Some of the bombs look hot," Sugar said.

Agent Brock paused. "Hot?"

Sugar nodded. "I wouldn't spend time in here until you get a bomb expert in."

"You all were in here," Brock said.

"We're all bomb experts," Archer said as he led his team out. They were free. The FBI hadn't taken their names or any other information. He figured if they needed something, they would contact Creed.

The drive back to San Diego took longer than he wanted. When he entered the room with Candace, a weight lifted from his shoulders.

"You're here," Candace said.

"You're safe." Archer moved to her but was too afraid to touch her. "How do you feel?"

"I'm okay. The pain medicine is great. I've had x-rays, and they are waiting to do an MRI if the x-rays turn out weird."

The door opened, and a man stepped in wearing a white coat. "Hello. Seems you saved us from a terrorist."

Archer narrowed his gaze at the man. Of course, this was supposed to be secret, so everyone would know. "Something like that."

"Don't be modest. I heard it on great authority. I'm friends with a few of the admirals on base. We're running this as a test operation for a terrorist attack, or that's what we're putting in the notes. This way, it will stay out of the media. The x-rays look good. You have cracked ribs, so no marathons or rough play. We need you to take it easy for two weeks and then get reevaluated. Your bruises will heal, and you'll be good to go in a few weeks. Don't overdo it, and we'll get you some medicine." The doctor turned to Archer and shook his hand. "I love how you SEAL guys take your work seriously. Thank you."

They shook hands with the doctor and then turned back to Candace. "When will she be able to go home?"

"I want to keep her overnight. In the morning, I'll reevaluate her and make sure she's well enough to take care of herself at home."

"I care for a baby during the day," Candace said.

"Hmm, you'll need some help. I'm sure the other Navy wives and husbands can pitch in."

"We'll have her covered, don't worry," Archer said.

The doctor took off, and Archer sat on the edge of the chair beside the bed. He clasped his hands together and rested his forehead on her arm. "God, Candace, I really thought I'd lost you."

"I thought I would die. I'd prepared to fight until the end."

Tears filled his eyes, but he brushed them away. "I'm not sure how to keep you safe."

"Archer." Candace's strong voice drew his attention. He stilled at the serious expression shining through the bruises and bumps. "I'm good. You don't have to keep me safe. This was a fluke, not something to ever happen again. Did you see the guns they had? They are a terrorist cell operating on our soil. If I hadn't been abducted, just think how many people would have died."

"But I can't lose you."

"Babe, you go off to other countries, operating

under terrible situations, and you do it to save us from a terrible end. I'll be fine. I'll be more aware of what's going on. Also, the terrorist cell will be shut down."

"I just—"

"No, we're not going to freak out and worry you sick over what happened. I trust you, and I trust the FBI to figure out how deep the cell went. Those people will be stopped."

Archer closed his eyes and blew out a breath. "You're such a strong woman."

"And you're a strong man. We'll get through this. You'll be able to live knowing I'm safe. I'll be safe, and you'll be safe, and we'll be okay."

He opened his eyes and stared at her. The fear he'd seen before, the unease she'd worn like a cloak, was gone. He brushed his hand over her forehead, leaning in to place a kiss on her nose.

"You seem different—stronger."

"I made a few decisions while I was being held captive. I don't want to live my life in fear. I know they tried to destroy me, but I can't let them. They hold no power over me now. I fought them, taking them down when I needed to. When your guys showed up, I may have been on my back, but I wasn't giving in to them."

"I'm proud of you."

Candace proved her strength once again. She'd been through a terrible situation and had come out stronger. He would encourage her to go to therapy, but she would be okay.

She closed her eyes and he let her rest. That night he slept in the chair beside her bed. She told him he didn't have to, but he wouldn't leave her side.

They were home from the hospital by eleven the next day, and he had to run to the base to take care of a few things. Creed had stopped by the hospital room the next morning and thanked Candace for fighting so hard. The FBI had found plans to blow up bases across the USA. They were starting here in California. They also found four other warehouses in Texas, North Carolina, one in Florida, and the last one in Virginia. The attacks would have happened on the same day. They were lucky.

Candace spent the day resting. That evening Sugar and Ella came over. Caroline, Fiona, Cheyenne, Summer, Jessyka, Alabama, and a few of the other Navy spouses were taking over Candace's position watching Ella until she recovered. They all were pitching in willing to take turns to help. Candace was blessed to have such good friends willing to help out. When she'd come to San Diego, she'd felt so alone, but now she had a family. They weren't Marines, but her Navy family was just as important as her buddies in the Marines had been. She still missed them, but she was thankful to have these people to support her.

Two weeks after she'd been abducted, she was called onto base with Adam and his team. They were led into the admiral's office. When the door opened and the admiral stepped in, the guys at her side stiffened and saluted. All of their everyday casualness they existed in was gone. These were Navy men through and through.

"At ease. I'm Admiral Guthrie, ma'am. I hear we have you to thank. I was out in Virginia earlier this week, and I saw what those terrorists had planned. They would have destroyed a couple of our ships and tried to kill as many men and women as possible. They planned to destroy bases in Texas and along the east coast. They had plans to blow up the White House."

"Jesus," Candace said under her breath.

"Exactly." Admiral Guthrie chuckled before he reached out and took her hand. "I know you're not Navy, but Marine. I wanted to give you this as a token of my appreciation. We can't publicly acknowledge your part or the SEALs' part in this operation, however, I want you all to know your dedication to the safety of the United States has been noted. Also, I have a house on Catalina for your use in two weekends. I've made sure you're all off-duty and have arranged transportation for you and stocked the refrigerator with beer. Enjoy your weekend."

The men laughed and shook the admiral's hand. Archer winked at her. Healing had started, leaving her lighter than before. Whatever had been in her way, keeping her from getting past the ordeal she'd suffered overseas, was gone. She'd had a couple of good sessions with her therapist, and she was better. Because of her injuries, she and Adam hadn't had sex, but she wanted to soon. Maybe, just maybe she'd be able to before they went to Catalina.

# CHAPTER 20

The transportation to the island Admiral Guthrie had supplied them with was a lovely yacht owned by a senator that picked them up from the dock. They had beer, and Candace had wine cooling in a bucket of ice. Archer stood next to Candace and watched as they approached the island.

"You're cool with me being with you guys?"

He looked down at her and lifted his hand, brushing her hair out of her face. "I like being with you."

"I won't cramp your style."

"Heck no. If anything, you'll give me more style. The guys like you and you fit in perfectly. Sugar brought Ella."

Candace chuckled. “She’s such a daddy’s girl. She loves him so much.”

“He loves her and is looking forward to spending the weekend taking care of her.”

“Dion is a good daddy.”

“You ever wonder about being a mom?” Archer held his breath as Candace turned from looking at the island.

“With Ella in my life, I have to admit the thought has entered my mind.”

“I mean other than Ella.”

Candace’s laugh filled him with wonder. “So did I.” She lifted on her toes and brushed a kiss over his jawline.

“Would you marry me?”

The question slipped out. He’d been planning on asking her once they were on the island after they’d spent the day playing and having fun. But right then, while they were alone at the bow of the yacht, it seemed like a good time to ask.

“Are you sure?”

“Babe, I am. You’re exactly what I need and what I want. I know your past and you know mine. You know how intense my job will be. I’m not a prize, I get that—”

“Oh, Adam, you are more than a prize. You’re an

honest, loving, caring man who is strong and isn't afraid to stand up for what is right. You're exactly the man I want to be with."

Archer smashed his lips against hers and kissed her like there was no tomorrow. He had the love of his life, and she wanted him.

The house was perfect. They spent the afternoon playing at the pool and hanging out. Black made burgers, and they built a fire in the pit on the back patio. The weather was just right, and the company was even better. At ten in the evening, Candace took his hand and led him to their bedroom. Not one of the guys said a word. They all stayed out by the fire drinking more beer while they talked about crazy missions and other things they'd done.

Candace was ready to have sex. Adam had been hesitant, but she needed to touch him. They both looked in on Ella, who was sleeping like the little princess she was.

When they stepped into their room, Candace tugged off her shirt and pants before Adam had turned around.

"Whoa, I didn't—"

"Be quiet and let me strip you." She wanted him so much she was already wet.

"Are you sure? I mean the doctor—"

"The doc says I'm fine. Just none of the rough stuff."

Adam drew in a sharp breath and groaned. "Jesus, Candace, how can I say no?"

"You're not supposed to." She tugged at his clothes, and he helped her with them, stripping down to his underwear.

"Shower first. I stink."

Her laughter filled the room. "Sure, we can do that, but I want to touch you while we're in there."

"You're making this hard."

She looked down and saw the ridge of his cock poking at his underwear. "I'm supposed to."

He pulled her close and ran his hands over her naked body. She was the most beautiful woman he'd ever seen. He was having a hard time keeping his focus during the shower. Desire to push her up against the wall and slide in almost overrode his senses.

She dropped to her knees and sucked him while he was rinsing his hair. He almost came.

"Fuck, I'm so close."

She stood and turned, sticking her ass out. "Then I suggest you get in me."

"Oh, God." Archer's hands shook as he reached for her. He needed Candace, but my God, he would do it in bed and show her how much he cherished her. Later, once she was healed, he would take her in the shower. He flipped off the water and grabbed the towels, handing one to Candace.

"What—"

"Bed, now," Archer barked.

"Nice," Candace purred.

He followed her to the bedroom and locked the door. She stretched out in the middle of the bed and laced her fingers behind her head as she spread her legs. Heat filled him. He was in heaven.

He moved fast, kissing just below her belly button before he made his way lower and licked up her pussy. She moaned as his tongue circled her clit. He used two fingers to part her lips before he licked up her center again. She shivered and arched into him as he sucked down on her. She was wet and tasted perfect. He licked and sucked, teasing her with his fingers until she cried out.

"Now, Adam!" Candace bucked against his mouth, and he moved fast, sliding into her.

This was heaven. They'd only done this once before, and she'd tortured him by tying him up. He would never tie her up, not with her past, but he would gladly submit to her again. Just the idea of her making him stay still made his desire burn hotter.

"Oh, damn." He ground out between clenched teeth. "I can't—"

Candace's fingers dug into his back, and he pumped in, barely holding onto his sanity. Her legs wrapped tighter around his hips. Her breasts were pressed up against his chest, teasing him. He needed relief. Then he looked down into her face, seeing the love he had for her reflected. He came hard, filling her with his cum. Soon they would do this to make a baby. Tears filled his eyes. He wanted a good future with her.

"Candace, you've made me the happiest man alive."

Her lips curved up. "I love you."

"I can't believe you want me as a husband and that you want to start a family with me. I'm nothing special."

"Oh, love, but you are. I feel so much for you. You're everything to me."

"And you're my everything."

He stayed buried in her, not wanting to let go. He knew soon enough the world would encroach. They would be called in to defend the USA, Candace would have to deal with Ella being sick or something, and the world would beg to be first. But nothing, not the military, not anyone else would ever come before his Candace.

"I'll love you until the end of time," Adam whispered.

"And I'll love you back."

His lips met hers in a fevered kiss, a promise of commitment. They had each other, and she was more than he'd ever hoped to have. She did more than complete him, she was his perfect lover, and he would cherish her until the day he died.

THE END

## ABOUT THE AUTHOR

Julia Bright is the author of the contemporary military romance Dark Eagle series and is an Operation Alpha Author. Julia lives in the south where "bless your heart" is an insult and "shut up" shows love. Julia has been reading since they could open a book and has taken the passion for words and combined it with the love of travel to create stories full of passion and excitement. If you love a good book with a fantastic happily ever after, you'll enjoy a Julia Bright novel. For a dash of paranormal romance and urban fantasy, pick up a book from Julia's USA Today Bestselling JS Bright pen name

facebook.com/AuthorJuliaBright
amazon.com/Julia-Bright/e
bookbub.com/authors/julia-bright

## OTHER BOOKS BY JULIA BRIGHT

**Special Forces: Operation Alpha**

*Saving Lorelei*

*Rescuing Amy*

*Saving Sloan*

**Seeking Justice**

*Justice for Amber*

*Searching for Keeley*

*Justice for Oswin*

*Safety for Eve*

**Dark Eagle Series**

*Survive The Fall*

*Live Past The Edge*

*Hold on Through the Pain*

**Storm Corp Series**

*Determined*

**Standalone Romance**

*Acting The Part*

*All Business*

*Just One Taste*

*There are many more books in this fan fiction world than listed here, for an up-to-date list go to www.AcesPress.com*

*You can also visit our Amazon page at:*
*http://www.amazon.com/author/operationalpha*

***Special Forces: Operation Alpha World***

Christie Adams: Charity's Heart
Denise Agnew: Dangerous to Hold
Shauna Allen: Awakening Aubrey
Brynne Asher: Blackburn
Linzi Baxter: Unlocking Dreams
Jennifer Becker: Hiding Catherine
Alice Bello: Shadowing Milly
Heather Blair: Rescue Me
Anna Blakely: Rescuing Gracelynn
Amy Briggs: Saving Sarah
Julia Bright: Saving Lorelei
Victoria Bright: Surviving Savage
Cara Carnes: Protecting Mari
Kendra Mei Chailyn: Beast
Melissa Kay Clarke: Rescuing Annabeth
Samantha A. Cole: Handling Haven
Sue Coletta: Hacked
Melissa Combs: Gallant

Anne Conley: Redemption for Misty
KaLyn Cooper: Rescuing Melina
Liz Crowe: Marking Mariah
Sarah Curtis: Securing the Odds
Jordan Dane: Redemption for Avery
Tarina Deaton: Found in the Lost
Aspen Drake, Intense
KL Donn: Unraveling Love
Riley Edwards: Protecting Olivia
PJ Fiala: Defending Sophie
Nicole Flockton: Protecting Maria
Michele Gwynn: Rescuing Emma
Casey Hagen: Shielding Nebraska
Desiree Holt: Protecting Maddie
Kathy Ivan: Saving Sarah
Kris Jacen, Be With Me
Jesse Jacobson: Protecting Honor
Silver James: Rescue Moon
Becca Jameson: Saving Sofia
Kate Kinsley: Protecting Ava
Heather Long: Securing Arizona
Gennita Low: No Protection
Kirsten Lynn: Joining Forces for Jesse
Margaret Madigan: Bang for the Buck
Kimberly McGath: The Predecessor
Rachel McNeely: The SEAL's Surprise Baby

KD Michaels: Saving Laura
Lynn Michaels, Rescuing Kyle
Wren Michaels: The Fox & The Hound
Kat Mizera: Protecting Bobbi
Keira Montclair, Wolf and the Wild Scots
Mary B Moore: Force Protection
LeTeisha Newton: Protecting Butterfly
Angela Nicole: Protecting the Donna
MJ Nightingale: Protecting Beauty
Sarah O'Rourke: Saving Liberty
Victoria Paige: Reclaiming Izabel
Anne L. Parks: Mason
Debra Parmley: Protecting Pippa
Lainey Reese: Protecting New York
TL Reeve and Michele Ryan: Extracting Mateo
Elena M. Reyes: Keeping Ava
Angela Rush: Charlotte
Rose Smith: Saving Satin
Jenika Snow: Protecting Lily
Lynne St. James: SEAL's Spitfire
Dee Stewart: Conner
Harley Stone: Rescuing Mercy
Jen Talty: Burning Desire
Reina Torres, Rescuing Hi'ilani
Megan Vernon: Protecting Us

***Police and Fire: Operation Alpha World***

Freya Barker: Burning for Autumn

Julia Bright, Justice for Amber

KaLyn Cooper: Justice for Gwen

Aspen Drake: Sheltering Emma

Deanndra Hall: Shelter for Sharla

Barb Han: Kace

EM Hayes: Gambling for Ashleigh

CM Steele: Guarding Hope

Reina Torres: Justice for Sloane

Stacey Wilk: Stage Fright

**Tarpley VFD Series**

Silver James, Fighting for Elena

Deanndra Hall, Fighting for Carly

Haven Rose, Fighting for Calliope

MJ Nightingale, Fighting for Jemma

TL Reeve, Fighting for Brittney

Nicole Flockton, Fighting for Nadia

***As you know, this book included at least one character from Susan Stoker's books. To check out more, see below.***

## SEAL of Protection: Legacy Series

*Securing Caite*

*Securing Brenae (novella)*

*Securing Sidney*

*Securing Piper*

*Securing Zoey*

*Securing Avery (May 2020)*

*Securing Kalee (Sept 2020)*

## Delta Team Two Series

*Shielding Gillian (Apr 2020)*

*Shielding Kinley (Aug 2020)*

*Shielding Aspen (Oct 2020)*

*Shielding Riley (Jan 2021)*

*Shielding Devyn (TBA)*

*Shielding Ember (TBA)*

*Shielding Sierra (TBA)*

## Delta Force Heroes Series

*Rescuing Rayne (FREE!)*

*Rescuing Aimee (novella)*
*Rescuing Emily*
*Rescuing Harley*
*Marrying Emily (novella)*
*Rescuing Kassie*
*Rescuing Bryn*
*Rescuing Casey*
*Rescuing Sadie (novella)*
*Rescuing Wendy*
*Rescuing Mary*
*Rescuing Macie (Novella)*

**Badge of Honor: Texas Heroes Series**

*Justice for Mackenzie (FREE!)*
*Justice for Mickie*
*Justice for Corrie*
*Justice for Laine (novella)*
*Shelter for Elizabeth*
*Justice for Boone*
*Shelter for Adeline*
*Shelter for Sophie*
*Justice for Erin*
*Justice for Milena*
*Shelter for Blythe*
*Justice for Hope*
*Shelter for Quinn*

*Shelter for Koren*
*Shelter for Penelope*

**SEAL of Protection Series**
*Protecting Caroline (FREE!)*
*Protecting Alabama*
*Protecting Fiona*
*Marrying Caroline (novella)*
*Protecting Summer*
*Protecting Cheyenne*
*Protecting Jessyka*
*Protecting Julie (novella)*
*Protecting Melody*
*Protecting the Future*
*Protecting Kiera (novella)*
*Protecting Alabama's Kids (novella)*
*Protecting Dakota*

*New York Times, USA Today* and *Wall Street Journal* Bestselling Author Susan Stoker has a heart as big as the state of Tennessee where she lives, but this all American girl has also spent the last fourteen years living in Missouri, California, Colorado, Indiana, and Texas. She's married to a retired Army man who now gets to follow *her* around the country.

www.stokeraces.com
www.AcesPress.com
susan@stokeraces.com

Made in the USA
Monee, IL
12 May 2020

30598433R00144